DANGEROUS FREEDOM

DANGEROUS FREEDOM

A NOVEL

BY

WILLIAM DEAN

DANGEROUS FREEDOM
©2021 by William Dean
All rights reserved

This is a work of fiction. All names, characters, places and incidents either are products of the author's imagination or are used fictitiously. No reference to any real person is intended or should be inferred. No part of this book may be used or reproduced in any manner without written permission except in the case of brief quotations embodied in critical articles and reviews.

Printed in the United States of America
Designed by 100 Covers

Published by Lonely Whale Press
Astoria, Oregon

ISBN: 978-1-7373452-0-6

In memory of my mother

Sittin' in the morning sun
I'll be sittin' when the evenin' comes
Watching the ships roll in
Then I watch 'em roll away again

Otis Redding

DANGEROUS FREEDOM

1

Bud heard the familiar music announcing the man's arrival – heavy shoes thumping a bass rhythm on concrete, the high notes of jingling steel keys. Checking the clock on the cinderblock wall, he scowled.

The prisoner absently stroked his whiskered chin as the uniformed guard appeared by his side.

"They're ready."

Refusing to be rushed, Bud placed his pencil on the table next to his legal pad, with its creased pages, scrawled notes and margin doodles, and gently closed the law book that had been the focus of his fierce attention.

"Coming, boss."

The numbered man stood, combed his curly mop of dark brown hair with his fingers and extended his hands without being asked to do so. Cold steel enveloped his wrists.

Guided by a firm hand on his shoulder, the inmate in baggy white coveralls and blue canvas slip-ons made his way out of the Idaho State Penitentiary law library, down a long Pine-Sol-scented passageway and through two security doors that buzzed open and slammed shut behind him with a guillotine-like thud.

The final barrier had a small window and the corrections officer peered through it before giving a practiced nod to the closed-circuit camera.

Bzzzz

"Here we go," the officer said in an aging Irishman's baritone, roughened by cheap cigars. He pulled with some effort and the heavy door swung open.

"Here goes nothing," Bud muttered.

Soon he was seated in a stark room that passed for a small auditorium. His bare wooden chair rested on an elevated platform that likely doubled as a stage.

Facing him, two men in suits and a woman in a dress with a floral scarf draped over her shoulders sat at a table dotted with piles of thick file folders – the life stories of dangerous men.

To his left he could see several rows of metal folding chairs, only one of which was occupied. His audience.

The convict didn't recognize anyone. It had been nearly 10 years since he'd been in the room. He wondered what it was used for besides bullshit like this. Take Your Daughter to Work Day? Trivia night?

His escort had disappeared behind the security door, but another guard – about 20 years younger and twice as menacing – stood against a wall cradling a shotgun, positioned to take Bud out should the need arise.

The beige prison in the tumbleweed desert south of Boise was a security expert's wet dream.

Ringing the two-story cellblocks and other structures were twin 12-foot-high chain-link fences topped with coils of flesh-slashing razor wire. In a barren strip between the barriers, salivating attack dogs prowled. Towering stands of light clusters covered every conceivable inch of ground and beyond them loomed seven watchtowers in which marksmen with high-powered rifles eagerly awaited a reason to shoot.

Escapes were rare. Most inmates who tried ended up dead.

As he sat on his chair, Bud had no such ambitions, although a younger version of himself once dreamed of nothing else.

"Good morning, Mr. Baker," the man in the middle said. "How are you today?"

"Peachy," Bud snarled, wrinkling his nose as if an offending odor had wafted his way.

"Good, good. Well, let's get right to it, shall we?"

He glanced at the stenographer, a thin woman in a cotton dress and librarian glasses. She smiled, signaling her readiness.

"This is the parole hearing for Wallace D. Baker, who is present. I am commission chairman Alex Cooper and with me today are commissioners Alice Witherspoon and Harley Johnson. We've all read the reports and are ready to proceed."

Cooper, wearing a double-breasted black suit and wielding a Mont Blanc pen that he frequently tapped on the table for emphasis, started with a dramatic recap. He spoke about a brazen robber who embarked on a one-man crime spree across a swath of the West that spanned four years, terrorizing dozens of people and culminating in the kidnapping of a woman at gunpoint in order to force her husband, a supermarket manager, to unlock the safe.

The robber was captured after a police chase and shootout in rural southwest Idaho that left a deputy dead, Cooper noted soberly.

The inmate yawned and noticed with some amusement that the grim men in the front row of the makeshift gallery disapproved.

A leather-skinned Marlboro Man in a wheat-colored cowboy hat clenched his fists. The others shot lasers with their angry, narrow eyes.

Cooper droned on for several more minutes before saying something that caught Bud's attention.

"… and the litigation, of course."

The candidate for parole straightened. This was the part of the reality show he wanted to hear. *The new stuff.*

After a rocky start to incarceration that involved sucker-punching a guard and spending six months in isolation, Bud had become something of a model prisoner. By the start of his fifth year and continuing to this day, his record had been clean. No more fights. No more contraband. No more willful rule-busting.

That was quite an accomplishment for a man who despised being told what to do and how to do it – especially by anyone with a badge – but it merely foreshadowed a much bigger transformation.

Bud learned to channel the raw power of his pent-up anger in a new direction. Dumbfounding everyone who had crossed his path, he became a champion for his fellow inmates.

Putting a largely untapped but keen intellect to use, the high school dropout studied the law while behind bars – voraciously, like a starving man at a banquet table. At the same time, he learned how to gather evidence, allowing his naturally gregarious self to emerge. What he gleaned from conversations with inmates and corrections officers, he applied to the few outdated law books available to him.

And then, on behalf of the 880 souls imprisoned in the desert, he did the inconceivable: He sued the state in federal court on constitutional grounds, claiming its flagship prison was overcrowded and lacking in basic services.

Somehow, some way, he won what would later be hailed by a criminal justice expert as "the single-most important prison reform case in Idaho history."

"We're keenly aware of your litigation in U.S. District Court … um … on behalf of the prison population," Cooper continued, tapping his pen on news clippings in front of him. "The new maximum-security prison is under construction as we speak."

Witherspoon whispered something in the chairman's ear.

"And your lawsuits that resulted in accreditation for the prison school and the expanded law library," he said. "That is in the report – along with Mr. Baker's more frivolous legal actions, such as the demand for a premium cable television package and smoking lounges."

Bud allowed himself a mischievous grin.

He'd been locked up for 25 years – half his life.

In the early '90s, he was a rampaging criminal who earned a place on the FBI's "Most Wanted" list instead of a diploma. The sentencing judge called him a "menace." Cops spit on him.

Now his scruffy beard was sprinkled with gray. There were lines on his face, and in a perverse way they only made a mug framed by thick, corkscrew curls even more handsome. But his kind, soft-brown eyes reflected a growing void in his soul.

With every passing year, his hopes of getting out, of tasting freedom once more, dimmed – until there was only darkness in the tunnel that passed for his existence.

There's zero chance of that changing today, he thought.

———

Bud's transformation to jailhouse lawyer had given him an almost mythical status behind bars.

With each courtroom victory, the tales grew.

There were many theories posited about Bud's motivation, but the truth was it had nothing to do with remorse or rehabilitation. The shaggy-haired prisoner in Unit 4 had not discovered Jesus either. He didn't even set out to improve the lot of his fellow inmates. Not at first anyway.

It really started with a food fight.

Tensions had been rising for weeks because cells were being double- and sometimes triple-bunked. There were long lines to use pay phones and see visitors. Angry white inmates were being warehoused next to angry black and brown inmates.

The fuse was lit on Super Bowl Sunday at 3:25 p.m. when the prison's cable TV went out. By dinner time, the mood had grown ugly. Officers began barking at the unruly cons and the cons were barking back.

Bud saw the Fritos fly, followed by hot dogs, and smiled. At least there would be some evening entertainment.

The riot lasted several hours and there were injuries on both sides, but what stuck in Bud's head was the snippet of conversation between corrections officers he overheard on the way back to his cell.

"There's too many of them. Too goddamn many," one said, breathing hard.

"And more coming in. Lots more," said the other.

"It's gonna only get worse if the state keeps ignoring this crowding. Mark my words."

"Yeah, but nobody gives a shit about these dirtbags, so here we are."

The post-riot lockdown lasted a week, giving Bud plenty of time to lie on his thin mattress and think. It was one thing for inmates to complain about prison conditions – it was another thing entirely for guards to agree it was a problem.

When the restrictions finally lifted, Bud managed to grab a seat in front of the one of the few computers available to inmates. He started reading up on prison overcrowding across the nation, which everyone seemed to agree was the inevitable result of a zero-tolerance war on drugs and ever-lengthening criminal penalties.

An idea started forming in his brain. In other states, corrections departments were being sued. Why not here?

He began his legal research with one goal in mind: He simply wanted the state of Idaho to suffer. He craved a chance to make his captors feel his pain. In a court of law, he'd be a human being, not a number.

Fueled by bitterness, he wrote to the Idaho chapter of the American Civil Liberties Union and, in an unwitting stroke of genius, did not beg for an attorney like all the other inmates. He merely asked the overburdened advocacy group what could be done about the dangerous conditions he was living in.

They wrote back with suggestions about how he could bring such a case in federal court, attaching a copy of a similar suit filed in New Jersey.

They didn't advise Bud to do it all himself, but that's exactly what he did. Prisoners, he soon learned, have a fundamental constitutional right to use the court system to address civil rights violations and often have no choice but to represent themselves in pro se petitions, despite the risk of harassment by prison officials.

A few weeks later, Bud drafted his first federal lawsuit. The complaint was a hot mess, peppered with misspellings and grammatical errors, written by hand on ruled paper like a middle schooler's homework assignment.

He mailed it to the ACLU to get some feedback and 36 hours later, a lawyer was in the prison visiting room, smiling as he clutched the black phone receiver on the other side of the Plexiglass.

"You have something here, Wallace," he said. "I think you should file."

"No shit?" the inmate said, surprised. "Call me Bud."

"We don't have any lawyers to assign to this but if the case is accepted by the court, we'll try to help you anyway we can."

"I could use it."

"Did you study law? This petition is a little rough around the edges, but your constitutional argument is solid."

"Nope. It's a whole new thing."

"Amazing," the lawyer said, shaking his head. "Well, keep it up. This could be big."

"Really?"

"Really. Want me to clean this up and file it for you? It would be my genuine pleasure."

"That would be great," Bud said. "I suppose they know where to reach me."

Wallace D. Baker v State of Idaho was filed in U.S. District Court in Boise the next day.

Bud had no idea what to expect and the suspense was agonizing, but after a couple of months had passed he received a letter from the court saying an initial hearing had been scheduled.

When he got to the end, he laughed. The powerful judge had authorized Bud to attend in person.

He had been locked up in a prison fortress for more than a decade, spending much of that time in maximum security.

But weeks later he found himself seated – although still in his jumpsuit and chains – in a spacious courtroom lined with rich mahogany paneling and huge oil paintings depicting scenes from the Old West.

The last time Bud had been in such a place, at his robbery trial, the judge called him "scum" and handed down a life sentence.

This time, the black-robed jurist with the silver mane perched above him referred to him politely as "Mr. Baker" and listened carefully to what he had to say.

A pair of assistant attorneys general argued against opening the door to a mandate that could cripple the state's budget. Calling the lawsuit "burdensome" and "unnecessary," they requested it be dismissed.

Bud was shocked when the Honorable William S. Sutton addressed him directly.

"Mr. Baker, what is your response?"

Rising to his feet, the notorious convict paused to gather his thoughts. He stroked his whiskers.

"Your Honor," he began, a slight tremble in his voice. "It seems to me the state isn't disputing crowding or anything else. They just don't want to do anything about it."

Bud glanced at the squirming lawyers at the table to his right.

"It's not my job to figure out how to fix things," he told the judge. "I guess that's yours. I'm just asking that you protect the rights of myself and every inmate in the joint, I mean penitentiary. Things are getting hot in there, with the riots and all. We need to be treated with human dignity, not like animals."

He sat down and then quickly jumped up again. "Uh, sorry. I meant to say thank you, your Honor."

When word spread behind prison walls that Bud was in court fighting against overcrowding, he become an instant hero.

Inmates he'd never met offered him extra food rations, smokes, drugs, booze – even conjugal visits with hookers paid to pose as wives. They slapped his back in the exercise yard like old friends and urged him to keep kicking The Man's ass.

Others flooded him with requests for legal help, convinced he could breathe new life into their groundless appeals. He did his best to avoid those rabbit holes. But when one of the friendlier officers quietly asked for advice on a potential grievance, he did a little research.

Bud didn't know what to make of it all. He set out to stick a shiv in the ribs of the prison system, make it bleed. Now, it appeared, he was doing something almost noble.

When the judge agreed to accept the overcrowding case and set a date for trial, Bud asked for another meeting with his mentor at the ACLU. He was nervous. The expectations were high, the pressure enormous.

"Bud, you caught the state's lawyers off-guard at that hearing. I think they underestimated you," the lawyer said. "They won't make the same mistake twice. They will fight this with everything they've got. The last thing the Republican governor wants in an election year is to spend millions on criminals."

"It's rehabilitation, ain't it?"

"That's a dirty word in this state. They want people who commit crimes to do hard time."

"Are you saying I'm gonna lose?"

"I'm telling you to do your homework. Preparing a case for trial is hard work. You'll need reliable, honest testimony. You'll need to obtain documents supporting your case and subpoena hostile witnesses, from the corrections director to the warden – or at least cross-examine them effectively. And that's just for starters."

"Crap. I only wanted to scare them."

"You have – and then some. But now you have to convince a judge to fix what's broken. You can do it."

"Can you help?"

"A little. We have a law library at our disposal, research tools. We can do that kind of work, and we'll be at the trial to assist if it gets that far, but everything else, I'm afraid, is up to you."

"You know what will happen to me here if I lose?" Bud whispered. He pantomimed a blade slicing his throat.

"Don't lose then," the lawyer said.

Bud wasted no time. For the next thirty days, he feverishly built his case. He prepped his witnesses, snared documents detailing the crowding problem through open records laws and his newfound subpoena powers, and began drafting his opening statement.

Less than a week before trial, he received a letter from a reporter at the Idaho Statesman, the daily newspaper in the capital city, requesting an interview. The journalist wrote that he was covering the case and wanted to profile the "prison plaintiff."

Bud was skeptical. Nobody outside the walls gave a damn about the people living within them, he knew.

Granting an interview was one of the stupidest things Bud could do. He was in over his head and likely to lose in humiliating fashion. He had tons of work left to do to prepare for trial and couldn't afford to waste any time.

For all he knew, the reporter could have been setting him up, intent on writing a hit piece on an inmate trying to game the system.

But Bud couldn't resist. He'd never been interviewed before.

He called the reporter collect from one of the cellblock's crowded pay phones. The next day, they met in the same glass-partitioned cubicle where Bud had talked to the ACLU lawyer.

"Nice to meet you, I'm Roger Sweet," the journalist said, pulling a notebook from his shoulder bag. "Like I said in the letter, I cover courts."

Bud said nothing, sizing up his inquisitor. Sweet looked to be in his early 30s, sporting a drooping mustache, tousled brown hair and a rumpled navy blazer with brass buttons.

"I'd like to ask you some questions about the trial, but maybe I can start with how you got here. Okay?"

How you got here.

There was a long pause as Bud weighed whether to reject such a personal intrusion and return to the law library. Instead, he remained seated and sighed.

"It's a long story, boss. How much time you got?"

"As much as they'll give me," Sweet said, tilting his head toward the guard standing nearby.

"Yeah, well, I'll answer what I want to answer. How 'bout that?"

"Perfect."

Sweet clicked his ballpoint pen and held it over the narrow white pages of his notebook. "Let's start at the beginning. Where were you born?"

With some reluctance, Bud's story trickled out: His childhood in Medford, Oregon. His father running out on his mother. The once-cheerful boy with good grades becoming sullen and difficult. The teenage delinquency. The ugly transformation to hardened criminal. The convict with the life sentence.

And now, the would-be reformer.

They wound up doing a series of interviews over several days, with the prisoner finding himself looking forward to each session. He watched in amazement as Sweet's notebook filled with ink, followed by another and another.

"Dude, I'm not that interesting," Bud said at one point as the journalist wrote furiously in his curious shorthand.

Sweet finished scrawling the quote and shook his cramping wrist. "I write down almost everything because they won't let me bring in a tape recorder. But it *is* interesting."

"What about all the cuss words?"

"I'll take those out. Sorry, family paper."

Bud could tell it wasn't going to be a hit piece, but the experience was still a bit unsettling.

He had been forced to relive his past and Sweet had a knack for getting to the root of things – the source of his deep-seated angst.

Bud had never been to a psychologist, but he figured this was about as close as he'd ever come. Talking so much about his feelings left him drained and a little dazed. Terrible things he'd walled off within himself were being unleashed.

After the final interview, tears stained his cheeks when the lights went out for the night. There had been a price to pay for getting his ego stroked.

The profile ran in the Sunday paper, starting on the front page with an artist's water-color sketch of Bud in his jumpsuit. Inside, the piece filled an entire page, wrapped around the infamous "Most Wanted" poster and sneering black-and-white prison mugshot.

The headline was "Idaho Jailhouse Lawyer Seeks Reforms."

Bud carefully read every word, including the praise from the ACLU and condemnation from law-and-order conservatives that Sweet warned would be part of the story. He loved it so much he taped it to the wall of his cell.

On the opening day of the trial, Bud saw Sweet take a seat in the front row of the gallery, bag slung over his tan sport coat, also rumpled. Several other reporters filed in moments later, drawn to the federal case by Sweet's story.

Even though it was a bench trial, Bud had been allowed to wear a long-sleeved white dress shirt and khakis. His ankles and hands were unshackled, but there were at least six Ada County sheriff's deputies fanned out in the courtroom.

The bailiff announced the entrance of the judge, who strode to the bench, head lowered like a bull, as everyone in the courtroom rose.

"Please be seated," Sutton declared.

Bud's opening statement did not go well. The words he had practiced aloud in his cell were jumbled by a bad case of nerves and he repeated himself far too much. At times, he mumbled and murmured, causing the judge to lean forward in hopes of hearing better.

Bud's first witness was Jerome "Ozzy" Smith, a hulking white man from the back woods of Louisiana.

"How many men are in your cell?" Bud asked, reading from his notes.

"Three," Smith said.

"I see, and how long have you been incarcerated at the Idaho State Penitentiary?"

"Fifteen years, six months and seven days."

"And when you were first incarcerated, how many cellmates did you have?"

"None. That happened later," Smith said in a Cajun drawl. "I got my first cellie five years ago. Last November, they moved in a nigger. Now that ain't right."

The judge frowned and Bud quickly continued. "Besides the color of the man's skin, what was it about having three to a cell that bothered you?"

"Waiting to take a piss. Being in the same room when they jerk off. But mostly, it was that black mother fucker. We got into some serious shit, brother."

"Mr. Baker, control your witness," the judge scolded.

Bud, nodding, changed the subject.

"The prison is supposed to offer programs to prepare you for society. What help have you been given?"

"Programs? Man, there ain't no *pro-grams.*"

"You're getting out soon. Are you saying the prison hasn't done a thing to help prepare you for life on the outside, like a job or a place to live?"

Smith burst into a fit of laughter that shook the witness stand.

"Your witness," Bud said to the assistant AG.

The well-dressed lawyer for the state approached Smith.

"What are you in for?"

"Rape, kidnapping, attempted murder."

"No further questions."

Days later, in his closing argument, Bud didn't mutter. With as much confidence as he could muster, he told the judge he'd proven the prison was an overcrowded powder keg that was seriously deficient in almost every way, even according to the state's own standards.

Sutton's monumental ruling came two days before Thanksgiving.

He found for the inmates, ordering sweeping reforms, including strict limits on cell-packing, a mandate for prison expansion and creation of a long list of rehabilitative and vocational programs – all to be overseen by an independent monitor charged with reporting back to the court in six-month intervals.

Bud read the news stories the next day in a daze. It felt like some kind of dream. He'd wake up at any moment to find it was all just his imagination.

Once that shock wore off, Bud came to realize that as an imprisoned David, his slingshot packed a punch. He hit the law books even harder, determined to force the prison system to at least try to put lawbreakers on the right path.

Over the next few years, Bud successfully sued the state several more times, forcing additional upgrades in the prison school and creation of a true law library, with complete sets of state and federal law books, computers and other research tools.

The library space soon became Bud's hangout.

When the hardback legal tomes arrived, he savored them like a fine wine, inhaling the smell of the stiff new pages, the glue of the binding. Reading the printed words was like tapping into a tiny current of electricity that couldn't be found anywhere else behind bars.

Corrections officers would often find him asleep at his table, one hand resting on a law book like a man being sworn in, a Black's Law Dictionary and his personal, well-thumbed paperback Webster's close by.

No prisoner had caused more trouble for the Department of Corrections in its history, but Bud had never been threatened. No one had ordered him to stop his legal work. He figured he had Sweet to thank for that. His profile had been raised, giving him at least some protection.

That all changed after the note.

One day, he returned to his cell to find a piece of paper neatly folded in half on his bed. He had no idea how it got there and he opened it with trepidation.

The message, printed by hand in capital letters, said: CHECK THE TRUST FUNDS.

Bud took that to mean the accounts set up to collect money earned by working inmates that could, in turn, be sent to loved ones on the outside or spent on a list of approved items, such as art supplies or books. The prison monitored the accounts to prevent large sums of cash from trading hands or being used to support the trafficking of drugs and other contraband.

Bud didn't have an account, but, curious and emboldened by his legal victories, he began asking around.

What he discovered alarmed him. A number of inmates said the balances in their accounts seemed to always be lower than they expected.

One said his brother on the outside deposited $1,000 for him, but the money never showed up. When he asked for an explanation from the warden's office, he was stonewalled.

Bud suspected the accounts were being embezzled, but he had no proof and investigating the warden and his staff while being at their mercy was extremely risky.

He decided to ask Sweet for advice. As always, the journalist patiently accepted the call.

"Hello, Bud. Still basking in your glory?"

"Actually, I have a question. About something very different."

"Okay, shoot."

Bud told him about the tip and his disturbing conversations with inmates.

"It seems to be true, but there's no way to prove it," he said. "And if I try to get records, they'll make my life a living hell."

"Any idea how much money is in these accounts?"

"A lot. A few hundred thousand at least."

"Wow," Sweet said, thinking. "Tell you what – get as many written statements from inmates as you can. See if they'll agree to using their names as part of an investigation. When you're done, send it to me. I'll see what I can do."

The legal affairs reporter never thought anything would come of it, but one day a fat envelope arrived from the prison. It was stuffed with handwritten statements by a dozen prisoners, some of them signed.

Sweet knew corruption when he saw it. He quickly drafted a major request for all financial records pertaining to the trust accounts going back five years.

As soon as the demand landed on the warden's desk, Bud was summoned to the prison administration building for the first time.

When he was seated in Joseph DiGionaro's office, the warden motioned for the pair of corrections officers to leave.

Leaning across his vast oak desk, between a brass bronco sculpture and a marble orb resting on a miniature stand, he glared at Bud.

"I know it's you."

The prisoner feigned ignorance, prompting DiGionaro to angrily cut him off.

"When you call a reporter, you think we aren't listening? You think I wouldn't be made aware that you're up to something? Your next big case?"

The veins on the warden's neck were bulging, but he leaned back in his padded leather chair, breathed deeply and clasped his hands behind his coiffed head.

"This is going to disappear. It's going to vanish because nobody gives a goddamn about scum like you."

"Not if money is miss—"

"*Shut up!* Say one more word and I'll have those men come in here and do some silencing."

Another deep breath.

"I want you to go back to your unit and tell everyone that no money is missing, not a fucking cent. Tell them it's all a big misunderstanding and you were wrong. You got that?"

Bud nodded.

"Good. If I hear you are pursuing this matter in any way, I will toss you in solitary for inciting a riot. No more talking to reporters or lawyers or anyone else. Do you understand me?"

Another nod.

"Now get the fuck out of my office."

DiGionaro pressed a button on his desk and the guards entered, grabbing Bud roughly by his shoulders and half-dragging him out.

Rattled by the threats, Bud followed the warden's orders and told the inmates who had risked retribution by giving him statements that he was dropping the matter. They did not take the news well. Several threatened to beat the jailhouse lawyer to death with his new law books.

Bud was too frightened to reach out to Sweet or take his calls.

A couple of weeks later, he was sitting in the library as usual. The wheezing, gray-haired prisoner charged with distributing magazines and mail shuffled toward him. He dropped the morning paper in front of Bud.

"Interesting reading today," the old-timer rasped before shuffling along.

Bud glanced at the front page. There it was, above the fold, splashed across five columns: "ISP Warden Ousted, Accused of Theft."

Stunned, he read Sweet's account of an ongoing federal investigation into an embezzlement scheme that had drained more than $250,000 from inmate trust accounts over six years.

DiGionaro, immediately fired by the governor, had just been arraigned on felony theft and conspiracy charges.

Other prison officials were being questioned by authorities, the story said.

"Shithouse mouse," was all Bud could say. "Shithouse fucking mouse."

———

That happened a few days before the parole hearing, where Bud now sat in judgment.

He noticed that the front edge of his chair had been scratched by countless fingernails. But he wasn't one of those anxious convicts. He never expected to get out.

He was a lifer.

"I applaud Mr. Baker's work in this area, which has clearly resulted in some notable improvements for the prison population," Witherspoon, the woman, was saying. "And I, for one, will take that into consideration."

"Of course," Cooper said dryly.

The chairman asked if anyone in the audience wished to speak and none did. They already had written to the panel demanding that Bud never get out.

They called him a "vicious criminal," a "monster" and a "danger to society." They said his jailhouse lawyer schtick was just another con.

"He should be hanged," one person wrote. "A leopard can't change his spots," expounded another.

The father of the young deputy killed in the shootout preceding Bud's arrest wrote a long letter, explaining in crushing detail his lingering sorrow. For good measure, he included a snapshot of his son's grave.

"Mr. Baker," Cooper asked, "do you believe you've been rehabilitated?"

"Absolutely," Bud said with a blank face. "One hundred percent."

"What has changed since your last hearing?"

"Changed? I've opened a law practice with more than 800 clients. Business is good."

Cooper frowned.

"I mean, what has changed in your life that makes you a better candidate for parole?"

"Nothing has changed," Bud snapped, unable to control a rising tide of resentment. "I'm still here. I haven't found God. I haven't had an epiphany. I can't change what I've done. I'm still here, only a lot older."

The trio at the table huddled briefly and then the chairman motioned to have Bud removed from the room.

"We'll inform you of our decision," he said.

An hour or so passed.

Bud was back in the law library in his favorite spot, catching up on some reading, when he heard the guard's heavy shoes and jingling keys.

When the prisoner looked up, he saw regret on the Irishman's ruddy face. He placed a beefy hand on Bud's shoulder but not to move him anywhere.

"Denied," he said.

2

The twentysomething man wearing mirrored sunglasses and a crisp gray uniform entered the grocery store shortly before 10 a.m. on a bright June day. He tipped his cap to a young woman waiting in the express lane closest to the wall.

She smiled shyly, twirling her long blonde hair.

He strode confidently to the manager's office and knocked on the door with the "Employees Only" sign.

"Wells Fargo," he announced.

The door cracked open and a slight, balding man with a nametag clipped to his green polo shirt eyed him suspiciously.

"You're early," the manager said, glancing at his watch. "Where's Charlie?"

"I don't know. I'm new."

"Never mind. Follow me."

The manager opened the door wide and walked over to a floor safe that was about the size of a washing machine. He twisted the dial back and forth until the tumblers aligned with an audible metallic click, then pulled open the thick steel door.

Inside were two bulging money bags – the overnight receipts. One by one, the manager handed the large canvas sacks to the man from the armored car company.

With a bag in each hand, Bud hesitated for a moment, then stepped toward the door.

"Wait!"

The imposter froze and slowly turned around. His gun hand tensed.

Here we go.

"You have to sign for it," the manager said, shaking his head. "Don't they tell new hires anything?"

The man in charge of the Lucky supermarket in Vallejo, California, whose framed photograph hung on the wall outside the office, centered above the other managers' portraits like Jesus and the apostles, rummaged through a desk drawer and pulled out papers that bore the Wells Fargo logo.

"Aha! Lucky for you I have extras."

He pulled a pen from his shirt pocket, made a few scribbles, then handed the paper to the trainee in the uniform.

"You sign there," he said, stabbing the spot with a bony finger.

Bud did as he was told, and the manager, looking like he was sucking on sour lemons, tore off a carbon.

"They really shouldn't send you guys out until you're trained."

"Sorry, sir. Appreciate the help."

Eager to move on to more pressing business, including a flood in the produce section that had just been announced on the store loudspeakers, the supermarket boss gave a dismissive wave.

Clutching bags stuffed with nearly $100,000 in cash, according to the receipt he'd just signed, Bud walked straight out of the glass-walled building as cool as could be.

When he reached the curb next to the shopping carts, he looked left and right. Nobody seemed to notice.

He put the bags and his cap in the trunk of a white Oldsmobile Cutlass parked near the east entrance, closest to the manager's office. He slipped on a black leather coat and climbed in. He turned the key in the ignition and the radio came to life – Led Zep blaring through the speakers.

You need coolin'
Baby I'm not foolin'
I'm gonna send you
Back to schoolin'

Just then, a 25,000-pound Wells Fargo armored truck with its slitted, three-inch-thick windows and gun ports pulled in front of the store, using the fire lane. The hardened steel rear doors swung open and a guard in a gray uniform stepped out.

Bud calmly rolled the Cutlass through the parking lot. In two minutes, he'd be on the interstate headed east. In less than four hours, he'd be over Donner Pass and in Nevada.

He saw the blonde from the checkout lane putting groceries in her Civic and gave her a wink.

She looked at the outlaw and smiled.

And then …

The woman is older.

She's screaming inside her house and Bud is telling her to shut up. But she won't stop, so he drags her down the stairs to the basement where the neighbors can't hear.

And he's tying her up and she keeps screaming, so he presses the barrel of the gun to her forehead and says, "Shut the fuck up, don't make me kill you!"

And then …

A man is on the floor, on his knees. The door to the safe is open and there's nothing inside, just an empty space.

Bud is yelling "Where's the money? Where's the goddamn money?" and the man on the floor is crying.

He pulls a snapshot of his wife and kids out of his wallet and he's begging, and Bud slaps it away and aims the gun.

Wheresthegoddamnmoneywheresthegoddamnmoney wheresthegoddamnmoney

And then …

———

Bud opened his eyes, shivering under his prison-issue blanket.

The hauntings were more frequent now.

The past he had tried for so long to wall off had broken through, like water spraying from cracks in a dam about to burst. He was 50 years old and he'd just been denied parole. There was little chance of ever getting out, at least with any time left to live. He knew that now.

The last strand of hope was gone.

He had become a prison anti-hero, respected by a smattering of liberal reformers on the outside. But he was anathema to the people in charge, and in America power is all that really matters. They would make sure he stayed caged for the rest of his days.

Bud shook his throbbing head as if trying to cast aside his demons.

Every night it seemed, another Wallace Baker True Crime Story played out on the movie screen in his brain. He wondered darkly if what he was experiencing was a preview of hell, in which sinners are forced to relive their worst transgressions over and over again.

He rolled off his bunk, bare feet hitting the cell's concrete floor. The cold was bracing, like a late fall breeze.

"Talkin' in your sleep again," came a voice from the top bunk.

"Go back to sleep," Bud said gruffly. "Don't want to hear your bullshit, Bobby G."

It was around 2 a.m. The main cellblock lights were still off and there were no sounds of anybody stirring.

"Crazy shit," the cellmate continued, now propped on an elbow. "Sounded like a confession."

Bud released a yellow stream into the chrome toilet that served as one of the cell's main furnishings.

"Confession, huh?" he said, flushing. "That's strange, for a man who's never stepped foot in a church."

"You were in a lot of pain. Screaming this and that. Surprised the goons didn't come."

"Ah, whatever." That was as close to an apology as Bud ever came.

"Worried about you, man. You ain't right in the head. Not lately anyways."

"Just a damn nightmare. I'm cool."

"If you say so."

Bud sat in the shadows, saying nothing more. After a while, he heard snores coming from the upper bunk and breathed a little easier. He didn't want Bobby G. to suffer on his account. Whatever was happening to him would pass, Bud told himself. Just like everything else in the joint.

Like all the months and years since his arrest.

A long, hard parade of passage.

When his mother, terminally ill with pancreatic cancer, wrote him a letter explaining the dire situation, he read it but didn't write back. He didn't ask permission to attend the funeral on a guarded furlough either.

That day just came and went, like all the rest. It was better not to care. That only led to heartbreak and feelings like that were a liability behind bars, a weakness to be exploited.

He remembered what the parole board chairman asked: *Do you believe you've been rehabilitated?*

Bud grunted. Is that even possible in such a hopeless place? No, he wasn't rehabilitated. Absolutely not. That's what he should've said.

And yet he knew he wasn't the same. The cocky armed robber locked up in 1996 bore no resemblance to the man he'd become – the self-taught ersatz lawyer. The celebrated reformer.

The truth is, if he got out now, if he was granted clemency, he wouldn't know what to do. Go straight and live free? Or rob again and die behind bars? It wasn't an easy choice. Thieving was all he really knew.

The inmate stared in a daze through the bars of his cell. Soon, there would be no way to block the memories. Cracks in the dam were spreading. He could feel it – an ominous rumbling in his brain.

Bud returned to his bunk and collapsed. He closed his eyes and squeezed his head with both hands but couldn't silence the voices.

You deserve to be here.

You deserve to be here.

You deserve to be here.

———

Bud was just a two-bit thief, picking pockets and mugging drunks, until he met a man in a Sacramento bar who worked for an armored car company.

Part of the man's job was picking up cash from supermarkets and taking it to banks for deposit.

Bud listened intently, prodding the off-duty guard to tell him more.

"Another round for my friend here," he yelled to the bartender.

There was so much cash being collected in grocery stores and so little security – the man told Bud after a couple of shots and a couple of beers – it was a miracle they weren't robbed more.

Bud insisted on walking him to his car after kindly picking up the tab.

"Thas cool," the man slurred. "What's your name again?"

"George."

"Tanks, George."

He helped the man into his cherry-red Mustang and while the drunkard was fumbling with the seat belt, Bud snatched the Wells Fargo uniform from the back seat.

"Drive safe now!" he called out as the car lurched away.

Bud grinned. He was about to hit the big time.

Preferring to work alone, he started by casing a local supermarket. He parked in the lot when it opened at 7 a.m. and stayed there, watching, until the armored truck arrived, pulling into the fire lane in front of the store's big glass windows.

He watched as one guard stepped out of the back compartment where the money is stored, looked both ways, and entered the supermarket. He timed how long it took for the man to return with the "coal bags."

Bud did this for a week, until he had the schedule down. He got as close as he could to the guard collecting the cash, known in the business as the "messenger" – even following him at a safe distance inside the store.

He took note of how the man carried himself, how he entered the manager's office, how he communicated with the driver in the truck, along with the gun holstered on his hip, the bulletproof vest under his uniform.

Bud's plan was to wait until just before the collection was due, impersonate a guard and walk away with the cash. In theory, he wouldn't have to use his gun or even threaten anyone.

He'd just hijack the cash and disappear.

The plan hatched by the 21-year-old worked flawlessly at first. Bud bounced from state to state, picking off busy supermarkets conveniently located off major highways providing premium escape routes.

He blew most of the money on working girls, cocaine and tequila. He spent freely because there was always the next job and the one after that. Not once had cops chased him. Not once had he fired a shot. He began to think he was invincible, or maybe just too clever to be caught.

But, of course, he was wrong.

Word of the robberies quickly spread across state lines. A security alert was issued nationwide by major supermarket chains, as well as by Wells Fargo, Loomis, Brinks and other armored car companies.

The FBI assigned several agents, who started by collecting in-store videos of the thief – Caucasian, medium build, about 5-foot-11, with curly brown hair and a mustache. The grainy image of Bud in his phony uniform was sent far and wide.

When Bud walked into a post office one day and discovered he had made the "Most Wanted" list and was the subject of a $500,000 cash reward, he should have stopped.

He laid low for a few months, flirting with the notion of maybe landing an honest job. But when his stash of cash started running dry, he grew antsy.

The young thief had grown accustomed to having lots of money – buying the finest liquor, reserving tables at the best steakhouses, staying in fancy hotels. He couldn't just give that up and go straight, work his ass off and make minimum wage. Where was the fun or thrill in that?

So, ignoring the voices of reason in his brain urgently shouting for his attention, he began casing another supermarket. It was the winter of 1996.

Back then, Nampa was a sprawling farm town in southwest Idaho best known for sugar beets and potatoes. The stench of beets cooking in the factories hung thick in the air, gagging anyone unaccustomed to it.

Bud didn't mind. He was drawn to the town by the presence of a bustling, super-sized Albertson's supermarket and the proximity of the interstate slicing through the snow-crusted fields about forty minutes east of Oregon.

He didn't know that the manager of the store was very much aware of the infamous "Supermarket Bandit." As added precautions, he had hired a security guard and doubled the number of surveillance cameras, inside and out. The supermarket still used an armored car service, but now the security guard was tasked with verifying the pick-up crew before they were allowed in the room with the safe. As a final measure, the armored car company had started mixing up the time of its stops.

The process was a bit cumbersome, but the Nampa supermarket had never been robbed. And the ambitious young manager – who had met millionaire founder Joe Albertson and was eager to advance his career in the fast-growing chain – intended to keep it that way.

Bud sat in his latest getaway vehicle, a two-tone Bronco with tinted windows, and shook his head.

He watched as a pot-bellied security guard chatted with the driver of the Loomis truck and checked his ID and paperwork. He saw the security employee follow the Loomis man into the supermarket and back out again. He noticed the added cameras. Now the parking lot was covered, too.

Bud should have reassessed the risks and walked away. There was no way his usual impersonation scheme would work.

There was a place he could go – a refuge in the wilderness.

A year earlier, he bought a log cabin and a few acres outside the town of Kodiak, Alaska. The house sat alone on a forested ridge overlooking a small lake filled with pristine, ice-blue water and cutthroat trout.

The lake had a long, narrow pier he had been to before. It was the place where his father taught him how to bait a hook.

Bud had never saved a dime and couldn't be less interested in settling down, but he found himself drawn by the magnetic power of a pleasant childhood memory.

He had held up a supermarket in the Pacific Northwest and scored big, so he decided to hide out in Alaska for a while. Once there, he got a sudden nostalgic urge to visit the lake recorded in his brain, so he took a ferry from Anchorage to Kodiak Island. He couldn't remember if the lake had a name, but he had enough details in his head to get directions. He decided to take a look.

He was astonished to find it exactly as he remembered, with the long pier and blue water, ringed by towering pines and majestic Sitka spruce.

"Gonna do some fishing, son?" a man called out.

"Don't have a pole."

"You can borrow one of mine," said the man, who stepped out of the woods. He was in his mid-70s, with wisps of snow-white hair and bright red suspenders.

"I came here once as a kid with my dad. He taught me to fish," Bud said.

"That's mighty fine," the jovial man said, motioning for his young visitor to take a grassy path up the slope. "Follow me to the cabin, I'll hook you up – no pun intended, ha ha."

They walked together for a minute or two and then entered a clearing, revealing the most beautiful cabin Bud had ever seen.

Elmore Dickens saw him admiring the place.

"It's for sale, if you're interested. I'm moving to town. Gettin' too damn old."

The cabin had a stone fireplace crowned with moose antlers, a compact kitchen built around a century-old cast-iron stove, a sun-drenched breakfast nook, a bathroom with a clawfoot tub and a surprisingly spacious bedroom.

But the best feature, Bud thought, was the cedar-planked front porch that ran the length of the house and overlooked the lake. He imagined himself rocking there, not a care in the world.

"Name me a price, young man, and it's yours."

"I'm sure it's worth a lot more than I can afford."

"Try me."

Bud had $125,000 in robbery loot in his hotel room that he hadn't spent yet. He made that the offer.

Dickens stuck out a hand. "Deal," he said.

They shook on it and Bud, ecstatic, hugged Dickens so hard the old man made odd, accordion-like noises.

Just like that, Bud had his refuge.

On a frigid winter day in southern Idaho, those thoughts entered his mind. He'd rob this oversized supermarket and return to Alaska for good, he decided.

He'd retire at the age of 25 and become a mountain man, chopping wood, making jerky and smoking fish. He'd invite his mother to visit. He'd find a woman who didn't mind the quiet and could appreciate how bright the stars shined at night.

After some in-store research that included studying the picture of the manager's smiling face on the wall, he returned to the Super 8 nearby. He grabbed the phone book and found the manager's home address.

The next day, Bud drove there and saw a lovely cottage with French-pane windows framed by white shutters and a waist-high picket fence out front. The mailbox by the gate was decorated with hand-painted flowers. In the driveway was a minivan and a tricycle with glittering streamers flowing from the handlebars.

He stayed in the Bronco down the street until a woman walked out, holding the hand of a young girl with pigtails and a sunny face. She looked to be about 4.

They drove off in the van and Bud followed for about six blocks, until they pulled into the parking lot of a day care.

Bud had found his window of opportunity. He checked his watch and recorded the time in his pocket notebook. Next to that entry he wrote "Get rope and duct tape."

The serial robber was taking it up a notch.

3

Karen Jones opened the front door and stepped inside, juggling her keys and two sacks of groceries. She placed the bulging paper bags on the tiled kitchen counter, then screamed.

A man was standing there, wearing a black ski mask. A chrome revolver was in one gloved hand. With the other, he put a finger to his lips.

"Quiet, Mrs. Jones," he advised calmly.

The terrified woman stared at the man in the mask, then at the gun, then back at the mask.

"What do you want?" she said in a voice that sounded like a squeak.

"I need you to take a seat," the intruder said, pulling over a straight-back wooden chair from the dining room table. When her nerves wouldn't allow her to move, he said more firmly, "*Now!*"

She obliged, watching the masked man with wide eyes.

"Here's the deal. I'm going to tie you up and take a picture. Then I'm going to leave. I'm going to show that picture to your husband and he's going to open up the store safe and give me the money. Understand?"

Jones nodded vigorously, chestnut hair tumbling over her eyes.

"If he doesn't open the safe, if he wants to be a hero, well, then we have a problem."

Bud bound her to the chair. He used so much rope it covered her from her neck to her ankles. It looked almost comical, but he needed a dramatic photo for his plan to succeed.

He ripped off a length of silver duct tape and placed it over her mouth. "Mmpphh," she protested.

"Sorry, but I can't have you yelling for help."

As tears rolled down the frightened victim's cheeks, Bud pulled a Polaroid camera from the sports bag he'd filled with burglar tools.

The flash went off and with a whirring noise the camera began spitting out the instant photo. Slowly the image came into focus: Portrait of a Horrified Woman.

Bud was pleased. He showed the picture to his victim.

"That should do the trick."

Bud went around the house pulling curtains closed and then cutting phone lines with the pocket knife he carried on his belt. When he returned, he gave the 35-year-old mother one last instruction.

"Just sit here and don't do anything stupid. There's a man with a rifle parked across the street. If you open that door in the next thirty minutes, he'll shoot you. Nod if you understand."

She bowed her head.

"Good. If you play it cool, this will all be over long before your daughter is done with preschool."

The mention of her daughter caused the woman to shake and sob. How did this robber know so much about her family?

Bud pulled off the mask as he stepped out into the cold. The pistol was tucked in the waistband of his jeans, concealed under a black leather coat.

He headed to the supermarket located a few miles away. He drove the speed limit, calmly and courteously, as he always did the day of a heist, as well-kept homes morphed into apartments and offices and then became the city's main commercial boulevard.

It was 9:05 a.m. The security guard started his shift at 9:45. The armored car would arrive at 10.

Plenty of time.

Bud parked the Bronco in the lot neighboring the Albertson's. It wasn't ideal, especially if things went south. But the spot he picked was just a brisk 25-second walk from the supermarket entrance and, most importantly, out of view of the security cameras.

The robber tucked his unruly hair under a blue Mariners ball cap, put on dark sunglasses and slung an empty nylon knapsack over one shoulder.

When he knocked on the supermarket manager's door, nobody answered. He suddenly became nervous. Standing in front of the door near the checkout lanes for more than a minute would draw unwanted attention.

Just as he was about to walk away, the man he recognized from the picture on the wall materialized at his side.

"Can I help you?" Chad Jones said with his best customer-service smile.

"There's a problem with one of your employees," Bud whispered. "Can we talk privately?"

Eyebrows raised, the manager unlocked the door and gestured for his guest to come in. Inside were a couple of no-frills metal desks, a row of file cabinets and the sturdy, squat floor safe.

Jones sat in a chair and invited Bud to do the same.

"Now, how can I help? What's the problem?" he asked earnestly, like a priest counseling newlyweds. He was in his late 30s, trim and athletic with a cleft chin and blond hair.

"This is the problem," Bud said, handing the manager the Polaroid.

"What th—?"

Bud cut him off. "Your wife is being held by one of my associates. If you cooperate, I'll tell him to leave. If you don't cooperate, he'll shoot her."

"*C-cooperate?* What do you mean?"

"It's pretty simple. You're going to open that safe over there and give me the money."

Bud opened his coat to reveal the handle of his gun.

"I need you to do that right now."

The robber glanced at his watch. It was 9:21, twenty-four minutes before the security guard was due.

"Please! Please don't hurt her!" the manager begged. "She's *pregnant!*"

"Congratulations," Bud said without changing expression. "Now open the fucking safe."

Jones scurried over to the steel box and after nervously flubbing the combination a couple of times, finally got it right. He pulled the door open, revealing three canvas money bags, stuffed and waiting to be taken to the bank.

Bud put the loot in his black knapsack and zipped it up. He slipped it over both shoulders, resembling a day hiker carrying picnic supplies.

"Now here's what we're gonna do—"

Bud was stopped by a sudden knock on the door. He pulled his gun and looked at the manager, who nervously shrugged.

Another knock.

"Chad, you there?" a man said from the other side.

Bud motioned for Jones to be quiet and waited for the sound of receding footsteps.

"Who the fuck was that?"

"That's Hank, the security guard. He must have started early; he usually checks in."

Bud's brows furrowed. He was being forced to improvise yet again and that wasn't his strong suit.

Screw this job!

"Okay, you're coming with me," he told the manager after quickly mulling things over. "We're going to step outside, and if we see Hank or anyone else, you're going to tell them you have a family emergency."

Jones gulped.

"You have the money. Just take the money," he squealed, squirming.

"I'd love to Chad, but the fucking security guard came to work early. So, now I'm going to drive you home."

"She's pregnant. Please don't hurt her."

"She'll be fine unless you do something stupid. Are you going to be stupid Chad, or are you going to be smart?"

"S-smart."

"Good choice, let's go."

They stepped out of the office. Jones, now perspiring heavily, led the way.

A woman in a polo shirt featuring the Albertson's blue-leaf logo took a step in their direction and the manager waved her away.

"Not now, Martha."

They ran into the security guard in his blue uniform in the vestibule where the shopping carts were stacked neatly in rows. A customer or two filed past, paying no attention.

"There you are," the guard said.

"Not now, Hank. Family emergency," Jones said, looking pale and pained.

The middle-aged, overfed guard followed them into the parking lot, much to Bud's chagrin.

"Anything I can do?" he shouted.

Prodded by the gun in his back, the manager didn't answer. Walking at an awkwardly swift pace, the pair made it across the snow-dusted lot and got in the Bronco.

The robber looked in his side mirror and saw the security guard, still standing in the lot, staring. He hoped the bastard wouldn't get suspicious and call the cops. This job was already complicated enough.

The drive to the Jones house took less than 10 minutes despite the slippery conditions.

Bud pulled the SUV in front, blocking the driveway. The minivan was still there – a good sign. He pointed the gun at his shaking hostage's face.

"Do you have a mobile phone?"

"Y-yes I do."

"Give it to me."

The manager dug in a coat pocket and produced his company-issued Nokia phone. He handed it to the robber.

"Don't call the police. Don't go to the neighbors. If you do, you and your wife will be shot. I have someone watching. They'll leave in thirty minutes, but until then, play it cool."

Jones didn't have to speak. The terror in his eyes said it all.

"Now get out."

The soon-to-be father of two stepped out into the frosty Idaho air, scented by smoke from logs burning in fireplaces. He ran to the front door and clumsily grabbed his keys, nearly dropping them in the snow.

When Jones disappeared inside the house, Bud drove away.

He steered the Bronco through the neighborhood using his practiced route, trying not to go too fast. He cursed as he hit a red light at the busy intersection that led to the freeway onramp.

Bud swore again when he remembered he didn't close the safe because of the interruption. Anyone entering the office would see it immediately.

It was 9:50. Jones was untying his wife. The guard was suspicious. The armored truck was en route to the store.

At any moment, he expected to hear police sirens.

"Fucking Nampa!" he yelled.

Cars ahead of him in the turn lane started moving and seconds later he was on Interstate 84 headed west.

His heart was racing almost as fast as the SUV's engine.

If he survived this accursed holdup, he thought, it would be a miracle.

4

The nightmares had become horror shows. Lately Bud would wake up, face twisted in fright, shirt soaked with sweat.

He was being chased by cops – always being chased. No matter how fast he'd drive or how many turns he made, they kept gaining on him.

There were people in the back seat and their hands were bound, their mouths taped. They were making an awful moaning noise that sounded like they'd been buried alive.

Bud would open his eyes, the chase would mercifully end, and the captives would vanish.

But the terror was always there, waiting for him, ready to resume the moment he dared to sleep.

The dam will break

The past will be the present

And I deserve to be here

Bobby G. told him he was no longer speaking words in his trance-like state – just making guttural, woeful sounds.

He knew it was true; he just didn't know why it was happening. He'd done some terrible things in his youth.

But why was his conscience punishing him now, so many years later, after he had finally done some good deeds?

Bud asked himself that before dawn one day when he was again shocked from his sleep, filled with dread. He got up to splash cool water on his face, then sat on the edge of his bed wondering what fate had in store for him.

The answer came quickly.

In the distance, he heard a steel door open and clang shut, followed by footsteps. Bud saw the dancing beam of a flashlight in the cellblock. The footsteps became louder.

And then two men stood in semi-darkness in front of the barred cell door. It slid open with a grinding sound.

One of the men shined his flashlight in Bud's face, causing him to wince and look away.

"Baker," the corrections officer said, "get dressed quick. You're coming with us."

Bud shielded his eyes with a hand. He knew all the guards who worked this part of the prison, and these two were new.

"Where are we going?" he said, still groggy from his night of torment. He got up and reached for his usual white coveralls.

"Not those," the guard with the light said. "Your court clothes."

"Guys, court isn't open this early. And besides, it's Sunday."

"Yeah, we know. Hurry up."

Bud slipped on his brown loafers, zipped up his khakis. He was still buttoning his plain white shirt when the pair hustled him into the corridor.

One of the inmates down the row yelled "Keep it down!" Everyone else, Bobby G. included, just kept snoring – a mix of sawing logs and sliding trombone sounds that came at the trio in waves.

Bud should have been alarmed by being rousted in the middle of the night, but he was too sleep-deprived to ask more questions.

The walk was a long one, taking them through secure doors and passageways, but finally they reached a large guard station he had never seen before.

Despite the hour – maybe 4 a.m.? – it was a busy place. There must have been a half-dozen officers in there, coming and going, checking paperwork. One guard glared at him, sipping coffee. Others gathered around a box of glazed donuts, making small talk.

Bud realized he wasn't wearing handcuffs, standard protocol for moving inmates around the prison.

"Wallace Baker," one of his handlers said into an intercom, and the last door buzzed open.

Suddenly, Bud was outside. *Really outside.* Not in a walled exercise yard.

He looked around in amazement, smiling like a madman.

A gentle snow was falling and flakes caught in the inmate's curly hair and on his eyebrows. He was standing in a large circular driveway at the front of the prison. A black van with no windows in back was idling.

One of the guards handed Bud an old leather jacket and a sealed envelope that looked like it had been through a spin cycle or three.

"Your personal items," he said.

The freezing cold had reached his brain and Bud slipped the coat on. It fit surprisingly well.

Bud stuffed the envelope in his pocket as a man in a black police uniform and matching Western-style hat approached.

"Let's go, Baker," he said. "This is your lucky day."

They climbed in the back of the slightly sinister-looking van, where another person in a gray fedora and thick wool overcoat was waiting. They sat on benches – Bud on one side, the strangers on the other.

The man in the uniform rapped on the window between the cargo space and the driver, and the vehicle began to move.

"I'm Commander Jenkins with the State Police," he said. "The governor has ordered your release."

Bud blinked stupidly.

What kind of cruel game is this?

"I just got denied parole," the convict said, wondering if this was another nightmare and he'd soon wake up in a familiar cold sweat.

"I don't repeat myself," Jenkins said, his face a blank slate of granite. "So listen carefully."

He reached into his chest pocket and handed Bud something. It was a bus ticket and a fifty-dollar bill.

Bud held the currency in his fingers. After two and a half decades behind bars, it was all the money he had. How long would it last?

"We're taking you to the station. You're going to get on the bus headed to the Oregon coast. I'll see that you do."

Jenkins paused. "Where you go from there is up to you."

"You mean I'm free? Forever? Just like that?"

The man in the fedora opened a briefcase and handed Bud a document.

"First you sign this."

Despite the dim light in the back of the van, Bud could see it was a waiver of some sort.

"It says you agree to never step foot in Idaho again. If you don't—."

"*I won't!*" Bud said, too eagerly. "I fucking hate Idaho! You can have your potatoes and Mormons."

The man in the fedora ignored the remark. So did Jenkins.

"*If you don't* ... you will be immediately arrested and returned to prison, where you will serve the remainder of your sentence with no chance of parole."

Bud slowly nodded.

"You also agree to drop any pending legal actions or investigations involving the state of Idaho and Corrections, and to never participate in any legal actions or investigations in the future.

"Finally, there is a stipulation that you have found a job and a place to live in ..." The man scanned his copy of the document. "... Kodiak, Alaska. Is that correct?"

"If that's what it says."

After breaking the news that he was in prison for robbery and other crimes, Bud had convinced Elmore Dickens to send a letter to the parole board making such a promise. But that was years ago. He had no idea if the offer to be his sponsor on the outside was still good.

"Sign on the last page," the man said, handing Bud a pen.

"Shouldn't I read it? I mean, it's four pages."

Fedora man exchanged glances with Jenkins. They clearly expected something like this from the jailhouse lawyer.

"We will be at the station in two minutes," Jenkins said. "If you don't sign by then, we're taking you back."

"S'okay, boss," Bud said meekly.

He scrawled his formal name on the signature line and handed the document to the man in the overcoat, who stashed it in his briefcase with a couple of snaps of its brass locks.

"I didn't catch your name."

"I'm with the governor's office. That's all you need to know."

The van rolled to a stop and in a flash the man with the briefcase was gone. Jenkins motioned for Bud to follow.

They were at a Greyhound station somewhere in Boise. It was snowing heavier now and the wind was picking up. He was grateful for his coat, which he zipped up to his neck.

"Your bus is here," Jenkins said.

Bud stuck out his hand and was surprised when the high-ranking cop took it.

"I'm really free?"

"That's right."

"I can't believe it. After all these years, why now?"

"Don't worry about that. It's a chance to start over — a gift. The only real question is whether you'll squander it," Jenkins said. "Now get on the bus."

Thinking again it was all a bad dream, he stumbled through the drifting powder to the big gray bus, disappearing in a cloud of steam and exhaust.

As Bud took his seat, he looked through his window and saw Jenkins standing by the van, watching, just as he had promised.

The bus rolled away in the darkness, headed west. There were only about a half-dozen people on board. A man two seats away was dozing, cradling cheap wine in a paper bag as if it was a baby.

The sun was up when the bus stopped outside a greasy spoon in Pendleton, Oregon. Before stepping out, the driver announced, "Breakfast, if you're hungry. Bathrooms inside. Thirty minutes."

Bud followed, realizing as a newly freed man that he could eat whenever and wherever it suited him. His first official act as an ex-con would be to eat a hearty meal. He was ravenous.

He sat at the counter and ordered a cup of black coffee with scrambled eggs, bacon, sausage and toast. He must have been really enjoying the meal because the waitress who refilled his mug said, "Another happy customer, I see."

She was a plain woman in her early 50s, plump, with sagging breasts and a prematurely aged face she did not bother to conceal with makeup. She chewed gum as she talked. Her apron was streaked with grease and ketchup. No matter what a customer said or asked of her, she'd pop her gum and say "No problem." If she wasn't providing an essential service for the road-weary and hungry, she'd be as interesting as wallpaper.

Bud, though, was enthralled. He hadn't seen a woman up close in 25 years, so every time the waitress hustled past on the other side of the counter, he had to look.

Her ponytail bobbed as she walked, brushing her bare neck. Her hips swayed just so. Her large buns shifted with each step like bouncing bowls of gravy.

The old-timer next to him in the fraying John Deere cap caught him ogling. He leaned over and whispered conspiratorially, "Meg has a great caboose."

Embarrassed, Bud asked for the check.

Minutes later, he was back on the bus, continuing his freedom ride. His geography was a little rusty, but he could see glimpses of the Columbia River and knew it would flow westward, to the Pacific.

His ticket was to Astoria, a fishing and logging town a few miles east of the mouth of the Columbia transitioning to arts and tourism, with a sprinkling of legal pot.

Bud had passed through once in his thieving days and decided it was too remote to rob. But it seemed nice enough, with a scenic waterfront and lively downtown, and gorgeous Victorian and Craftsman homes perched high on hills overlooking the port and its watery parade of cargo ships.

Having grown up in Oregon, Bud knew the white man's history of Astoria. It began in 1792, when Robert Gray, an American merchant sea captain, explored a mighty river while sailing the Pacific and named it the Columbia, after his ship.

In 1805, the Lewis and Clark Expedition reached roughly the same spot, ending an epic, 2,000-mile westward journey. But while Meriwether Lewis and William Clark built a fort, Astoria wouldn't become the first permanent American settlement west of the Rockies until six years later, when New York financier John Jacob Astor, the town's namesake, established a fur-trading outpost. The presence of the Pacific Fur Company drew trappers, but soon they were followed by sturdy pioneers, then rugged fishermen and lumbermen, and finally immigrants pursuing their dreams.

The history books Bud read didn't mention Astoria's bawdy period, with its rowdy saloons, dance halls and prostitutes, or its slow transition starting in the 1920s to a more cultured city dubbed "Little San Francisco."

Bud had no idea how much Astoria had changed while he was imprisoned. Fisher Poets still told their tales of a gritty life at sea, but most of the riverside canneries were gone, turned into tourist attractions. The fishing fleet had shrunk, augmented by cruise ships. The stars of the future were now baristas and brewmasters, actors and artisans.

Blissfully ignorant, the newly freed man figured he'd snag a job on a fishing boat or in a cannery and quickly earn enough money to make his way north, where a log cabin awaited and nobody would tell him what to do.

Leaning back in his seat, he thought, sadly, there was no one waiting for him. There would be no cake, no balloons, no tears of joy.

His mother was dead, his father long gone and he had no other relatives he was aware of. He had no friends to look up, either. He never bothered to make any.

He'd slept with a lot of women but usually only for a night or two. Now he couldn't remember any of their names.

The bus rumbled west on a ribbon of asphalt. By evening he'd be at his destination.

He'd never felt so alone.

———

Sweet played the phone message three times. He couldn't believe what he was hearing.

It was Bud, calling around sunrise.

"Hey, this is your old pal Bud. I've been released! I can't believe it either, but they fucking did it! They're calling us back on the bus now, so I got to go. Headed to the Oregon coast, man. I just had to let you know. I can't believe it. I'm free and I don't know how to act. *I'm a free man!*"

The fact that Bud wasn't calling collect lent credence to his story, as did the background sounds of forks scraping plates and people chatting.

The reporter had never heard of a prisoner, especially a notorious one, getting freed in such a manner – before dawn, completely under the radar. But there was nothing about Bud and his exploits that was ordinary.

Sweet's well-honed curiosity was stirring. Why would such a lock-'em-up state do such a thing?

He scrolled through his iPhone contacts and dialed the private number to the governor's press secretary.

"This is Farley Fellows."

"Hello, Farley, sorry if this isn't a good time."

"No, it's fine, Roger. What's up?"

"I just got a call from Wallace "Bud" Baker. Says he's been released from the ISP. Know anything about that?"

The phone went dead for about a minute. Sweet flipped his notebook open.

"I can't talk about that," Fellows finally said.

"Well, he's either released or he's not. Can you confirm?"

"Call Corrections. We have no comment."

"Farley, if Baker's been released, I'll have to write a story. Seems to me the governor's office would have to be pulling the strings on this one."

"Off the record?"

Sweet sighed. "Can't. Not on this."

"Jesus, Roger. I can tell you something, but it's deep background. You can't attribute it to me or the office."

The reporter reluctantly agreed. Another long pause followed.

"This thing came out of left field. We knew the governor was pissed about those never-ending court mandates to fund prison construction and programs, but one day he just said he wants Baker out. As in, out of prison, out of the state, for good. We tried to talk him out of it. He had just been denied parole, for Chrissakes."

"So, in the dead of night, he has a high-profile inmate put on a bus bound for Oregon?"

"Exactly."

"Hmm. What's to keep Baker from fighting the prison system from the outside?"

"We had him sign a waiver."

"A *waiver*? And he did?"

"Wouldn't you?"

"I suppose so … but the last suit Baker filed was two years ago and he lost. What got the governor so hot now?

"You don't know? I thought you and Bud were friends."

Sweet snorted. "It's hard to be friends with someone who's behind bars. I can't exactly invite him over for tea and biscuits."

"The last straw was the trust fund business and the firing. The warden was a close personal friend of the governor. It ticked him off that Baker made him do it."

"I was the one who broke the story, Farley."

"It's common knowledge that your inside source was Baker. But, hey, good work. He's been released, right?"

"Why no public announcement? Why the middle of the night?"

"The governor didn't want Baker to come off looking like a champion who brought the state to its knees. That's pretty much exactly what he said. That's all I have for you. Gotta run."

Sweet hung up and called Corrections. An official confirmed Bud's release but declined further comment.

After a few more interviews, Sweet began to type. He called out to the city editor, who was pouring coffee from a Thermos.

"They released Bud Baker!" Sweet bellowed. "I've got the story."

"You can make replate," the editor yelled back. "Type fast. We'll need it for the web right away!"

Less than forty minutes later, Sweet filed his piece, slated for a hastily cleared space on the front page. It began:

Wallace "Bud" Baker, the Idaho State Penitentiary inmate credited with reforming the prison system from the inside, was quietly released early Thursday.

"I'm a free man," Baker, 50, said in a phone call to the Idaho Statesman.

The Corrections Department confirmed the highly unusual release but declined further comment.

A spokesman for Gov. John P. Samuels did not immediately respond to a request for comment. The release of a high-profile prisoner would typically be approved by the governor's office, sources said.

Baker had recently been denied parole for a third time by the state parole board.

He had served 25 years of a life sentence for a series of armed robberies in the 1990s in five Western states. In recent years, the jailhouse lawyer gained fame for his successful class-action lawsuits against Corrections that have resulted in major reforms, including new prison construction.

In his early morning call to the Statesman, Baker said he was puzzled by his surprise release. He said he was about to board a bus bound for the Oregon coast.

"I can't believe it," he said. "I'm free and I don't know how to act."

Sweet was reading the replate edition at his desk when his phone rang. He readied his notebook, figuring it was one of his sources calling back.

Instead, a stranger was on the line. An older man with a dusty, graveyard voice.

"I just read your damn story online," the caller said with disgust. "Why don't you tell the truth?"

"Excuse me?"

"This Baker is a violent thug. He caused a man to die, terrorized good people. But you bleeding hearts don't care about that, do you? You've made him into some goddamn hero. He's no hero. He's a stone-cold killer – and he has to pay."

"Sir, I'm sorry you—"

The caller cut Sweet off.

"Yeah, you're sorry alright. You're the sorriest excuse for a newsman I've ever seen. You swallowed this B.S. hook, line and sinker. Prison 'reformer,' my ass. Playing you like a fiddle. But like I said, he'll get his. And soon."

The phone went dead.

Sweet was used to harsh reader reaction – some preferred that he not include an accused person's defense in his court stories – but this call gave him shivers.

The reporter nearest to him overheard some of the rant.

"What was *that* about?" she asked.

"Oh, probably nothing," Sweet said. "Just some old kook."

5

As a free man, Bud quickly discovered how hard life could be.

He arrived in Astoria in the dead of winter with $38.50 to his name, no change of clothes, no place to stay. His beard had reverted to castaway status, his white man's Afro resembled an overgrown hedge and his body odor was overpowering.

When he finally opened the envelope containing his personal effects, he found a broken pair of mirrored sunglasses, a wallet that was empty save for a long-expired driver's license, a used tube of Chapstick and a foil-wrapped Trojan condom. He put the condom in the wallet and slid it into the back pocket of his pants.

He was hungry and homeless and horny. The trifecta of misery.

The first night in town, despite temperatures dipping into the low-40s, he slept on a park bench a short walk from the waterfront. He vowed to start looking for work first thing in the morning, starting with crab boats and salmon processors. All he needed was a handful of paychecks to get himself a used 4x4 and journey north to Alaska.

Bud was jarred awake shortly before dawn by a loud barking noise.

Rubbing sleep from his eyes, he wondered why so many dogs were on the loose. He got up to investigate and was surprised by the true source of the racket.

Scores of sea lions had taken over a private pier nearby, forming a giant pile of flesh and flippers. The marine mammals bellowed at each other in mock protest as they rolled about, using each other's bodies for warmth.

For years, Bud would soon learn, the Port of Astoria had struggled to wrangle the protected creatures to keep them from sinking boats, destroying docks or harassing recreational anglers. But all of the measures, from flashing lights to high-powered water hoses — even a boat shaped like a whale that was supposed to scare off the seals — had failed.

The whiskered animals always figured out a way to keep their colony perched comfortably on the waterfront. They were at ease on the piers and floating platforms because their chief predators — orcas and sharks — didn't venture upriver. They adapted smartly to the presence of humans, raiding nets cast by fishing boats and robbing anglers of their catches. When the tourists gawked, they didn't seem to mind. In fact, they put on something of a show.

Bud enjoyed the spectacle immensely.

Sitting on the gray boards of a long pier, he watched the blubbery critters alternately frolic and snooze. He admired, with a touch of envy, how free and fearless the animals seemed to be.

After giving himself a short pep talk, he headed over to a public restroom nearby to get ready for some job-hunting. The ex-con cleaned himself up as best he could, tossing sink water on his face and armpits. He was grateful there were no mirrors. He hadn't groomed himself in days.

Bud spent the next three hours looking for a temporary job, talking to any commercial fishing boat captain and cannery boss he could find.

The outlook was bleak. Astoria's cannery row, the one he remembered from his youth, was gone. One cannery had been turned into a craft brewery, another a museum with a restaurant and coffee shop. Still another had been converted into a boutique hotel and spa.

There were few working seafood processors left and they weren't hiring, or at least they weren't hiring Bud. He took the bus to nearby Warrenton, where Pac-West Seafoods had a big processing plant.

"It doesn't matter what the job is," he told the manager. "I just need work."

The man eyed Bud suspiciously.

"I only hire Mexicans," he said.

Bud ignored the discriminatory hiring practice. He looked at the men and women working the canning and packing lines and saw that what the man said was true.

"Hey boss," he said, "I'll be real. I just got outta the joint. I need a job for a few months. Can you help me out?"

The manager spit on the floor. "I'm not a charity."

With that, he stomped away to cuss at his workers in Spanglish.

Bud fared no better with the crusty sea captains. Stormy weather and a lingering dispute over the wholesale price of sweet Dungeness crab had grounded the fleet for weeks and they were in a sour mood.

One of them grabbed the prospective crew member's hands and sneered.

"Those aren't working hands," the skipper declared.

"Just give me a chance. I'll work as hard as any man," Bud pleaded, to no avail.

By then it was midday and Bud's stomach was growling. He walked over to a riverside restaurant called Mo's and ordered a cup of clam chowder and bread to go. His meager savings continued to shrink.

He returned to his sea lion-viewing spot and devoured his meal, using his fingers to wipe the last creamy drops off the Styrofoam soup container.

Bud watched couples, hand in hand, walking along the boardwalk. An egret perched nobly on a chunk of driftwood, ignoring the swooping seagulls. The sun had broken through the morning fog, warming his cheeks and turning the river a deep blue.

His adrenalin-like euphoria over getting out of prison had dried up, but the pleasant scene raised his spirits.

An old song about a man sitting alone on the San Francisco waterfront after a long trek from Georgia popped into his head. He began to whistle, just like in the song.

"That's good," a voice from behind said as he finished. "Otis Redding, 'Dock of the Bay.'"

"You're right," Bud said, turning around.

It was a pretty woman in a pink wool coat, matching scarf wrapped loosely around her neck. She had twinkling, sea-green eyes. Her wavy red hair was blowing in the breeze. She looked like a mermaid, Bud thought.

"1968?" she asked. "I took a rock appreciation class in college."

"Think so."

"I was always confused by the whistling part. It seemed too happy for such a sad song."

"You're wrong about that. It's not sad."

The woman frowned, wrinkling her freckled nose. "It's about a lonely, depressed man. It's practically suicidal."

"Or … a man who fell on hard times, eager to start over. That makes it hopeful."

The woman smiled – a lovely, captivating smile. She seemed to know Bud was talking about himself.

"Redding died in a plane crash before that song was released," she said, continuing the banter. "That's also sad."

"Yeah, but it was a monster hit, so … kind of a silver lining?"

"Perhaps," she said, looking him over in a kind way. "You may want to wander over to the church on Franklin. They have showers."

She added: "And scissors."

"Everybody keeps telling me that. Thanks."

"Well, you do look *outdoorsy*."

"That's better than 'shiftless drifter.'"

"Oh, much better."

Amused, she gave a small wave with a gloved hand and walked off in the direction of downtown.

He admired how she moved – slower and smoother than most people, almost gliding, like she was floating on currents of air.

A floating mermaid.

He didn't get her name, but he didn't kick himself for failing to do so. She was definitely out of his league. Probably married to boot. And besides, he looked like shit.

Bud spent the rest of the day continuing his job hunt on the waterfront, but he kept striking out.

He'd try the lumber companies next. Business seemed to be booming, judging by all the fully-loaded logging trucks thundering through town and across the bridges. Becoming a lumberjack wouldn't be half bad, with all that fresh air. Besides they always seemed to eat well and chicks seemed to dig them.

It never occurred to Bud that his age might be a hindrance. He didn't think like someone facing middle age. In his mind, he was much younger.

The freezing wind was picking up, nipping at his face and fingers. It was late in the afternoon, and he still had no place to live. He stopped at a pharmacy for a few basic toiletries, then at a thrift shop for a pair of jeans, underwear, socks and a T-shirt. He opened his wallet and cringed: He had less than twenty dollars left.

His surprise release from prison, he now realized, came with a major downside. Most convicts were released to halfway houses, where they could be slowly reintegrated into society. Some had sponsors who would give them jobs and a place to stay.

Bud had no safety net.

All he really knew was how to steal and that would only lead him back to prison. How long could he last without a job and a roof over his head?

He found himself trudging up the hill to the church everyone had been talking about. Several other "outdoorsy" men had formed a line outside a side door.

Bud read the plaque on the front of the building proudly saying First Christian was erected in 1916, with its red-brick walls and sweeping front steps leading to tall oak doors framed by white columns. An aluminum-sided spire with a chrome cross topped the structure. It was pleasant-looking, but as churches go, almost humble.

The church held Sunday services, but its focus of late was serving the area's growing homeless population, offering cots, meals and counseling, Bud quickly discovered.

Feeling a bit ashamed, he joined the line under a stained-glass window depicting a biblical scene he didn't recognize and was soon ushered inside by a cheerful, matronly woman.

"You're new. Welcome. What do you need today?"

"A bed would be nice."

"And a shower?"

He nodded.

Jesus, how bad do I smell?

She handed him a bar of soap and a cheap white towel and directed him to the communal showers in the basement, located off a small dressing area. He hung up his coat and shed his filthy clothes, stuffing them in a cubbyhole.

When he was done, everything but his jacket, near-empty wallet and shoes was gone. Wearing his towel, he brushed his teeth and edged his beard with a razor, looking slightly more presentable. Then he put on his new clothes and stepped into the hallway.

The woman who greeted him was waiting.

"That's better," she said. "Your clothes are being washed. We serve dinner in two hours. In the meantime, we usually do some intake – information for our files."

She saw the reluctance on Bud's face and quickly added: "It helps us keep our grant from the city. We're one of the only shelters on the north coast and the need is so great."

Bud consented to the formality. The woman seemed relieved.

"I'll send in the social worker. You can wait there, in the pastor's office."

He stepped into an unassuming room with a desk and a table surrounded by a few folding chairs. A picture of a glowing Christ was on one wall. Another featured a quote from Martin Luther King Jr.

Bud was reading it when the door opened.

"The whistler!"

It was the woman he'd met earlier by the water.

This time she was wearing black jeans and a cream-colored sweater that revealed an attractive figure. Her hair was pulled back and a pen was lodged behind one ear. Her lips shined with gloss.

"You took my advice, I see," she said, directing Bud to the table. "Except for the scissors."

"One step at a time," Bud said, grinning. "So, you're a social worker, not a music critic?"

"I am. I work here in the afternoon; mornings at the jail. I prefer being here."

"Why's that?"

"A little less tragic, I guess. There's more anger and desperation at the jail."

Bud knew exactly what she meant.

"My name is Josephine Summers. Most people call me Jo Jo."

She stuck out her hand and Bud grasped it, enjoying the smoothness of her milky skin. He saw that she wasn't wearing a wedding ring.

"I'm Bud."

"Bud? That's a name you give a German shepherd who brings you beer from the fridge. What's your real name?"

"Wallace, but I've never cared much for it."

"Bud it is then." She had the pen in her hand and made a note. "You have a last name?"

"Baker, Bud Baker."

They talked for a while, with Jo Jo posing questions from a form attached to a clipboard. She was pleasant enough, but Bud detected a tinge of sadness in her eyes.

He recapped his failed attempts at finding work and afterward she offered a compliment, saying that most people who came to the church had given up trying.

"Truth is, Astoria is like any small town. It's all about who you know. Nobody advertises jobs. It's strictly word of mouth."

That explained why the "help wanted" column in the local paper was so short, he thought.

She looked at Bud intently and said, "You haven't been homeless for long."

"How can you tell?"

"You're too pale."

"So are you."

"Ah, yes, but that's my Scotch-Irish heritage. What's your excuse?"

Bud laughed nervously. She was getting dangerously close to asking whether he'd been in jail. That was something he didn't want to share. Especially the part about the life sentence.

"Hey, mind if I get a little shut-eye? I heard there are beds here."

"That's true. The Warming Center. I'll take you."

They walked through a hallway to a large meeting room that had been converted into sleeping quarters. Rows of military-style cots with blankets and pillows now filled the space from wall to wall.

"By midnight, they'll be mostly filled," she said. "Take any bed you like. They ring a bell when supper's ready. It's not gourmet cuisine, but it's filling."

"Thank you, Jo Jo."

"Nice to meet you. We'll talk again later."

Bud dropped heavily onto the nearest cot and closed his eyes. It was his second night of freedom and he was jobless and in a homeless shelter, wearing castoff clothes.

At least one good thing had happened, though. He had met a pretty girl.

He hoped he'd dream about mermaids, but he wasn't that lucky.

6

The flashing blue lights made him do a double-take.

Although he didn't keep count of his daylight heists, Bud guessed that the Nampa job had been preceded by at least 15 others in California, Oregon, Washington, Nevada and other parts of Idaho.

The FBI had been on his trail for a few years, but not once had he been in real danger of capture. He thought he was too cunning, but the truth was he had just been preternaturally lucky.

And now, for the first time, the bandit was being chased.

"Goddamn it!"

The cops were less than a quarter-mile behind and gaining. He looked at his speedometer and saw he was going 90. They were probably doing 95.

Bud started weaving through traffic, but the Bronco was already at its limit, judging by the vibrations he was feeling. He glanced in the back and could see the knapsack filled with cash bouncing on the seat.

He couldn't outrun them. And even if he did, when he reached the Oregon border, troopers would likely be waiting with a barricade and shotguns.

Hank! I know it was you!

Soon, they'd put a helicopter in the air and then it would be game over. There'd be no hiding then. He rolled down his window and looked skyward but couldn't see or hear anything.

The outlaw realized that the worst thing he could do was stay on the freeway. He had to get off the road, and he had to do it fast.

Bud waited for I-84 to curve to the right and then swerved onto an exit ramp as fast as he could. He raced through a stop sign and barreled toward a wooded area where he could get some cover.

The red-and-white Bronco steamed across a frozen potato field and skidded sideways to a halt next to a stand of lodgepole pines.

Then he waited.

He heard the sirens and prayed the police would keep rocketing down the highway, passing him by.

His prayer wasn't answered. Three patrol cars took the exit and headed straight for him.

Bud swore and grabbed the revolver from the glove box. He held the loaded gun across his chest as the sirens' wails grew louder.

So this is how it ends.

He thought about grabbing the knapsack and running wild through the trees. But it was too late, the police cruisers were within 50 yards of him now.

Bud's grip on the gun tightened. His index finger curled around the trigger.

Pulsing blue light painted his face.

Through the trees he could see the cops' faces.

And then … in a flash … they were gone.

Bud exhaled slowly as the lights dimmed and the sirens faded. The patrol cars had disappeared down a country road. They had been fooled, but not for long. He knew they would discover their mistake and double back in short order.

He stepped out of the Bronco, slipped the bag with the money over his shoulders and began picking his way through the woods, trying to stay out of sight.

As he had predicted, a line of patrol cars roared back down the road. Soon, they would find the empty SUV and the real manhunt would begin. They'd know he was on foot and alone.

He doubled his pace and, after slipping through underbrush and trees, came upon a clearing. There was a farmhouse in the distance. He could see a tractor rumbling nearby and a station wagon he could steal.

Bud crept through the field, trying not to be seen. He made it to the passenger side of the car just as the front door of the house creaked open. He heard footsteps and from his crouching position near the front fender he could see a woman crossing the yard, carrying a metal tub.

She was singing "Amazing Grace."

Bud didn't want to interrupt, but he had to. At any moment, the cops would arrive. He needed that car.

Keeping his gun tucked away, he rose from behind the station wagon and said, "Excuse me, ma'am."

The woman jumped with a shriek and promptly crumpled to the ground, scattering the branches she'd gathered for kindling. The outlaw ran over and saw she had fainted.

Bud searched the car but couldn't find the keys. He ran into the house and found them hanging on a hook near the stove. On his way out, he grabbed a denim jacket and a ball cap from a coat tree.

The woman was coming to as Bud drove away.

There was only a half-tank of gas, but that was enough. He just needed to get out of the search zone, find someplace to hole up for the night and let it all blow over.

He'd head south to rural Owyhee County – bordered by both Nevada and Oregon – where there was plenty of room to get lost for a while.

A few miles down the road he came upon a police car. It was parked to the side, lights flashing, and an officer was outside, flagging the wagon down.

Bud had put on the farmer's coat and hat. Sliding the gun under his seat, he rolled to a stop.

"What can I do for you, officer?" Bud said, pretending to smile.

"We have an armed suspect on the run," the cop said, scanning the inside of the car. "See anyone suspicious?"

"Can't say that I have."

The cop asked where he was headed.

"Nowhere, really. Just taking a little drive. My wife doesn't like me being around on laundry day."

"Son, you best be getting back home. There's a dangerous man on the loose, and it's not good to leave your wife unprotected."

"You're right, officer. I'll do that."

"And lock your doors. You can't be too careful."

"Will do. Thanks."

Instead, Bud kept driving south. It was getting dark when he reached a tiny Western-themed hamlet tucked on a broad plain near the Boise Mountains. He spotted an abandoned barn and pulled the station wagon inside and shut the big doors.

He resolved to spend the night in the old hay loft, staying out of sight.

But then he heard the music.

A band was playing classic rock at a bar nearby, on the town's only commercial block. They were really crushing it and Bud found himself tapping to the beat.

It wouldn't hurt to stop in and have a beer, he thought, his cockiness returning. *Cops wouldn't be searching this far out.*

Wearing his leather jacket and knapsack, he headed to the Wild Horse Tavern. The band was playing a decent version of "Hey Joe" by Hendrix.

I'm goin' way down south
Way down where I can be free
Ain't no one gonna find me

The long-haired musicians were shoehorned into a corner by the front window. Twenty or so people were dancing near the stage, forcing Bud to walk sideways to make his way to the bar.

All the stools were taken, but he found a small space by the wall where he could order a brew and check his bag with the bartender. He had just taken a frothy sip when a girl in red cowboy boots and a fringed mini skirt approached.

"Buy me a drink?"

Bud laughed as she stood there, swaying to the beat, oblivious to the fact that the song was about a man who gunned down his cheating girlfriend. She was blonde, in her early 20s, wearing a white leather top that showed some impressive cleavage.

"Sure. What are you drinking?"

"Bacardi and Coke with a lime." She smiled and began twirling to the beat, sending her fringe flying.

After scanning the front of the tavern for any sign of cops, Bud handed her the drink. She immediately drained half of it through a straw.

"Haven't seen you around. I remember all the cute guys," she said with a lopsided grin.

"Just passing through. What's the name of this town anyway?"

The girl thought that was hilarious. She erupted into a gale of laughter that involved spitting out some of her rum.

Bud stood there expressionless. He wasn't in on the joke apparently.

"This ain't no *town*. This wide spot in the road is Two Springs, Idaho, population 500, not counting the cows. No one comes here unless they have to, pretty much."

"Well, I'm here, the music is good and I think you're pretty. What's your name?"

"Carrie. What's yours?"

"George."

She leaned closer.

"George, wanna dance?"

The band had moved on to a Creedence medley, so Bud found himself dancing to "Born on the Bayou." He grabbed Carrie by the waist, pulling her close.

Two drinks later, they kissed and Carrie suggested they go to her place.

She was half-drunk and starting to slur her words, but Bud kept looking at those amazing breasts and decided that if she was still conscious in the next hour he'd fuck her.

Carrie talked nonstop as they walked. She lived with a roommate in a small house two blocks off Main Street, she said. They worked together, waitressing at Two Springs' only diner.

She was a prominent rancher's daughter and still received an allowance.

"Isn't that hilarious?" she said, unlocking the front door. "But that's Daddy for you."

As they stepped inside, Bud stubbed his toe on a coffee table and cursed. The house was completely dark.

"Where's your roommate?" he asked as a light clicked on in a back bedroom.

"Oh, Sue's at the bar," she called out. "She's dating the guitarist. Hey, handsome, come over here!"

Bud did as he was told and saw Carrie sprawled on the bed. Her top was off but she'd kept her boots on.

He dropped his jeans and slid onto the bed, slipping his arm under her bare back. He kissed her neck and worked his way to her nipples.

Carrie moaned and squeezed Bud's cock through his boxers.

He pulled off her panties and moved between her legs, pressing his body against hers.

"Ride me, cowboy," she said.

Again, Bud did as he was told.

———

Hours later, the outlaw rolled out of bed, admiring the naked ass of the girl he'd made love to.

The morning sun was filtering through the curtains, bronzing her flawless skin. There was an artistic quality to the pose – nude, with the folded sheet draped just so across her legs.

He padded his way to the kitchen and poured himself a glass of water. He felt an urgency to leave, to get across the border to a place where he could breathe easier.

The wilds of Alaska beckoned. With more than $125,000 in his bag, it was time for the outlaw to retire.

Then he saw a deputy through the kitchen window.

The uniformed cop was walking through a field behind the house, searching for clues. Bud jumped out of sight and peered again.

Now there were two deputies prowling in the back.

They must have found the car.

Bud hustled over to the front window and peeked through the drapes. Two more deputies were walking up the street. He watched as they stopped at the house next door and rapped on the door.

"Hey, baby," a sleepy voice said from behind.

Bud turned and covered Carrie's lips with his hand.

"Don't answer the door. I've got to run, but I'll be back. Don't answer the door."

"But—"

Carrie watched in disbelief as Bud ran into the bedroom and opened the window. It was freezing outside but he didn't have time to get dressed.

She followed.

"George, what's going on?"

There was a loud knock on the door. A man shouted "Police!"

"Don't answer that," Bud repeated. "And hide *that.*"

He pointed at his knapsack.

Carrie nodded dumbly as the man at the door yelled a second time, "Police! Open the door!"

Bud grabbed his gun and scrambled out the window, wearing only his boxers.

He dropped to the half-frozen ground. The cops searching the back field had their backs to him. He decided to sprint to a huge oak where he could take cover, let the searchers pass.

He was nearly there when a deputy suddenly appeared in front of him.

"Here he is!" the cop yelled.

Bud turned on a dime and began running back toward the street. Deputies seemed to be popping up everywhere — at least a half-dozen. They were drawing their weapons.

The next few seconds were a blur. Bud, panicked, began running aimlessly in a large circle to avoid the growing number of cops.

"He's got a gun!" someone yelled.

A series of loud pops followed as the lawmen opened fire.

Bullets began whizzing by Bud, some from the front, some from behind. One grazed his cheek, another his right leg. He dove to the ground, hugging the wild grass, but the bullets kept flying.

"He's down!" one deputy shouted.

Then Bud heard something strange: "Officer down! Officer down! Hold your fire!!"

Three deputies pounced on Bud's back. They yanked his hands behind him so hard one of his shoulders nearly dislocated.

"Cop killer," one of them snarled. He spit in Bud's face as he was pulled to his knees.

He could see a deputy bleeding profusely from his neck about forty feet away. His head was on the lap of another deputy, who was crying.

"I didn't shoot!" the handcuffed outlaw protested, only to be greeted with a punch in the jaw that nearly knocked him out.

They hustled him into the back of a patrol car.

From the back seat, he could see the knapsack and his jacket being taken out of the house. The gun he had dropped in the field was in a clear-plastic evidence bag.

Carrie appeared on the front porch in a terrycloth robe, arms folded across her chest.

She's worried about me, Bud thought.

Then she flipped him off.

7

Bud prowled the waterfront with a vengeance, pursuing any job that paid. Even the grizzled old salts who kept turning him down came to appreciate his earnest desire.

"Sorry, Bud. Nothing today," they'd say.

In the restaurants and hotels downtown, there was another familiar refrain.

"Come back in the summer when the tourists are here," they'd tell him.

It was his bad fortune to be stranded in Astoria in winter when jobs were scarce and only locals walked the streets.

Legs dangling over the water, Bud sat on his favorite pier, where he had started giving the sea lions names. He didn't mind the cold; it kept his senses sharp.

Downriver about a mile loomed the Astoria Bridge, a long, green-steel link to Washington state. Cars and trucks rolled across headed north, but Bud, alas, couldn't join them.

He tossed the last of his fish and chips to Big Mama, who barked in delight, standing on her back flippers.

"You're welcome Mama, but have some dignity," Bud said. "You're not a circus seal."

From behind, he heard a voice call out, "Oh boy!"

He turned and saw Jo Jo standing on the boardwalk. There was no mistaking the flaming hair.

"When you talk to wild animals that way you're either Dr. Doolittle or you're losing your mind," she said, walking over. "I think I prefer the whistling."

"You missed that part of the show."

Jo Jo surprised Bud by sitting next to him.

"I see you here every day when I'm out walking. You picked a good spot. How many sea lions have you named?"

"Well, let's see. There's Big Mama and Big Daddy, they're the oldest, I think. And Flubber, Dizzy, Whiskey and Tango."

"Great names."

"Whiskey and Dizzy get confused sometimes."

"I bet. And Tango?"

"He's the only one who's graceful on land."

"And Flubber is clumsy?"

"That's right! Always stepping on the others to get to the warmest part of the pile. He's the one who starts that huge ruckus in the middle of the night."

"Mystery solved! Alert the media!"

Jo Jo laughed in a way that made her emerald eyes glow. Bud did his best not to stare.

"How's the employment search going?"

"Zilch. A few odd jobs here and there, day laborer stuff. Whatever I make, I spend right away."

"Well, at least you finally got a haircut."

Bud did an impression of a preening fashion model.

"I'm jealous of your curls," she said. "Mine cost me dearly."

Seagulls swooped in noisily to grab the lone French fry Big Mama didn't eat. After a brief silence, Jo Jo gave Bud some amazing news.

"I actually was looking for you today. I think I have a job you might like – and maybe a place to live."

"A place of my own, without the snoring and strange smells?"

"Maybe. And you may still be able to hear your flippered friends at night."

"And to what do I owe this winter miracle?"

"I know someone."

She got up and dusted off her slacks.

"Meet me at the church when you're done pacing the waterfront. I'll introduce you to Harry."

"Okay. You doing this as a friend or a social worker?"

"A little of both."

She walked down the pier toward town, floating in her special way over the old, weathered boards.

Bud watched her go for a long minute, then resumed his whistling – a bit too upbeat for a down-on-his-luck man.

———

Harry Golden liked Bud right away.

He prided himself on being able to look a man straight in the eyes and see his soul, just as plain as could be.

What he saw in Bud he didn't say, but he took him to be somebody in the midst of turning his life around and that was a good thing. A very good thing indeed.

Golden could relate. He had rebounded several times, twice after bitter divorces that drained his coffers and a third time after he became an angry drunk who had lost all his friends.

Now, at the age of 77, he had been reborn, even becoming a respected figure in town.

Through a series of shrewd investments, he built a small real estate empire. He acquired a number of old buildings in Astoria's core, most of them rundown and on the verge of collapse. Then, much to the delight of the city council, he restored them to their original grandeur – or at least a better incarnation of what they had been.

Golden's efforts were touted by the chamber of commerce as well as prickly historic preservationists, but what mattered most to the aging businessman was the money that started rolling in. At his two refurbished hotels, the Essex and Eloise, he doubled the daily room rate, but the tourists still came in droves. At his commercial buildings, he boosted the rent, but nobody left. In fact, he had a waiting list.

His latest acquisition was The Royal.

The three-story apartment building, erected in 1903, had fallen on hard times, becoming a disreputable flophouse. Like all of Golden's newly purchased properties, it required a lot of fixing up. Paint was peeling inside and out. Eaves were rotting. The roof was patchy and on the verge of collapse. Cast-iron waste lines were cracking.

The Royal was a royal disaster, but Golden had a knack for recognizing potential. He'd stand across the street and squint for a while, envisioning the transformation of a building from eyesore to eye-pleasing. Most of the time he made it come true.

For years, he joined the crews doing the rehab work on his buildings. But his back now ached and his knees and wrists were too arthritic to wield hammers and saws.

The Royal was perched on the first slope south of downtown, a block from the church where Bud had been sleeping. He had walked by it many times, admiring the progress of the restoration.

As he and Jo Jo walked up the concrete steps to the lobby, stepping onto the big "R" engraved in the center, construction sounds echoed through the building.

A long drop cloth ran through the lobby and up the stairs to one of the apartments. Down it came Golden, wearing dirty jeans and a T-shirt splashed with paints of various hues. His wild gray hair looked electrified.

Jo Jo shook her head.

"You told me you weren't doing that kind of work anymore," she scolded.

"I'm not, Jo, I swear. It's just that some of these guys don't know their ass from a tea kettle."

"Harry, this is Bud. Bud, Harry."

Golden pulled off a filthy glove and the men shook hands for what seemed like an eternity.

"Jo tells me you're looking for work," the businessman said finally. "And that I can trust you."

"Yes, boss."

"This here is The Royal, once the queen of the district." He pointed out the carved moldings in the high-ceilinged lobby.

"This is turn-of-the-century craftsmanship. All the floors are old-growth Doug fir, the beams are the best cedar you've ever seen – a foot thick. The bones are good, it's the rest of her that needs work."

Golden paused and stepped closer to Bud, their noses just a couple of feet apart.

"There are eight apartments – or at least, there will be. We've finished work on four. A couple of teachers and their kids, and the new town librarian are moving in next week.

"But I'm a busy man. I need someone I trust to manage this place for me. When a lightbulb needs changing or a toilet is clogged, I need them to call you, not me."

"I can do that," Bud said, repeating a line he'd uttered hundreds of times since arriving in town.

"Have you ever worked as a handyman?"

"Not exactly, but I can do almost anything if you've got the tools."

Golden pursed his lips as he thought about the man standing before him. Bud hoped he wouldn't inspect his hands for callouses like the fishing boat skippers did.

"I'm not going to ask you to tell me your story," Golden said softly. "You can tell me some day if you like. All I ask is that you work hard and honest."

"Yes, sir."

"Do you drink a lot?"

"No, sir."

"That's fine. Too much drinking can destroy a man."

Bud shifted his weight nervously.

"Jo says you've been sleeping down the street, at the church."

"That's right. I—"

"Don't need to hear your story, like I said. We all have our ups and downs, but if Jo vouches for you, that means a whole lot. I can let you stay here, in one of the top apartments. It needs a little work, but if you're handy like you say, you shouldn't mind. Instead of rent, do that work and you can stay as long as you'd like. For managing the building, I'll pay you $500 a month."

"That's fine," Bud said, suddenly elated.

"But if I get any complaints about you goofing off or not being courteous and such, you're gone. I will fire you on the spot. Understand?"

"Yes, boss."

Golden's stern demeanor vanished in a flash. He slapped Bud on the back.

"Well, that's that then. You can start tomorrow."

"Thank you! That's great!"

Golden gave Jo Jo a wink.

"We'll see if you feel that way after you carry groceries and gallons of paint up three and a half flights of stairs. There's no elevator, son."

Golden dug in his pocket and handed Bud the keys marked "No. 8."

"I've got a planning board meeting to get to," the businessman said, hustling past Bud and Jo Jo. "Make yourselves at home."

"Dressed like that?" Jo Jo said, but it was too late. Golden had disappeared down the street.

The way to Bud's apartment was around the back through a rear door. Compared to the ornate front, this half of the building was plain, like an old servants' entrance. They climbed the painted wood stairs to the top floor.

When they reached the landing, Jo Jo looked like she hadn't been climbing at all. Bud was hunched over, panting.

"That whole groceries thing might kill me," he said.

They stepped inside and were greeted by piles of construction debris, from broken tile to empty paint cans. Cigarette butts and a few empty Budweiser bottles were scattered on the floor. The kitchen sink was missing. A ceiling light was dangling by its wires.

"Jesus Christ," Bud breathed. "I was hoping he was kidding. 'A little work?'"

Jo Jo shook her head. "Home sweet home."

But they stepped into the living room where a dazzling view filled a series of three windows. They looked over the rooftops of downtown buildings to the blue water shining in the sun.

The third floor had its advantages after all.

"No more complaining about the stairs," Jo Jo said. "This is beautiful."

"Well, we haven't seen the bathroom."

The social worker looked at her watch. "Ooh, gotta go. Meeting at the jail."

Bud reached out and squeezed her hand for a second.

"We should celebrate. Can I take you out tonight?"

"I don't think so. Besides, you're broke."

"I didn't say I was *paying* for it," he said with a devilish grin, flashing his dimples. "Come on, it'll be fun."

"You're kinda my client."

"Not anymore. I'm a building manager-slash-handyman with a luxury view apartment."

Jo Jo rolled her eyes.

"You've got a lot of work to do. Get yourself – and this place – together. Besides, you don't want anything to do with me."

"Oh yeah? Why's that?"

She gave him a mirthless smile.

"I'm in a dark place."

She headed down the stairs at a gallop before Bud could think of what to say to such a strange comment.

Then he surveyed the kitchen devastation and sighed.

I do have a lot of work to do.

"Where's that damn sink?"

<h1 style="text-align:center">8</h1>

Two truths soon revealed themselves. One was that Bud knew next to nothing about carpentry, plumbing, electrical work, refinishing and painting. The other was that he learned incredibly fast.

The Astor Library was just two blocks downhill from The Royal, which helped immensely.

Bud discovered the do-it-yourself section and checked out as many books as possible. When a special need arose – an almost daily happening – he'd camp out in the aisle, turning pages and taking notes. When the library was closed, he'd peruse YouTube videos on an old Dell computer – one of Golden's hand-me-downs.

The jailhouse lawyer was becoming a self-taught handyman.

His ace in the hole was the construction crew toiling a couple of floors down. Through flattery and self-deprecation – and their concern that the man in No. 8 would either flood the building or burn it down – Bud got them to regularly inspect his work.

Their verdicts were often blunt.

"That's wrong," one man said of his wiring. "Do it like this."

"Sloppy," another said of his staining. "Brush this way."

Through mostly trial and error, he gradually deciphered the secrets of remodeling. He figured out how to use a compound miter saw and high-powered floor sander, learned the hard way to measure twice and cut once. Most importantly, he knew when to surrender and start over.

Soon, there was a working sink in the kitchen. The bathroom boasted a new toilet and shower head. A restored antique light hung in the living room and plaster walls were patched and repainted. Throughout the flat, the freshly sanded fir floors, stained a rich walnut brown, gleamed.

Bud's confidence in being able to handle basic chores in the building was growing, which was good since tenants had started moving in.

Golden had faith in him, and he didn't want to let his benefactor down.

It took Bud a full day to haul all the construction debris and trash out of the one-bedroom apartment. Another day was spent doing a thorough cleaning, scrubbing every dust-covered surface.

But despite all that hard work, it was just an empty place.

He had almost no furniture, other than a small cafe table and chair he found dumped on the curb and a cot borrowed from the church. When he played music on his garage sale radio, the sound echoed off the bare walls.

Filling the place would normally be a slow process for a man with almost no money, but he felt some urgency.

No longer in a hurry to get to Alaska, he now wanted to prove to Jo Jo that he was worthy of her affection. The apartment renovation, he thought, would help him clear some of those hurdles.

So, when Golden stopped by for a look one day, Bud was anxious.

The building owner did his best to draw out the suspense. He walked around, running his fingers over the new molding. He ran the faucets, turned on the lights. He crouched down low, despite his bad knees, to inspect the floors up close.

Finally, he returned to the kitchen and sat heavily on Bud's reclaimed chair.

"I'm impressed. You did well with my money."

"Whew."

"Hearing some good things from the renters, too. They seem to like you."

Golden surveyed the barren apartment, using his unmatched powers of imagination.

"You know, if you get some decent furniture in here, some curtains, art on the walls … this place could be nice. Very nice."

He looked at Bud strangely, then added, "I think Jo would like it."

"You think I stand a chance? She went to college. I didn't make it past 10th grade."

"Hard to say. Passionate women – and most redheads are, from my experience – can be stubborn, fiercely independent and hard to predict. A lot of successful men have tried to win her, but I see the way she is around you."

He smiled, as if remembering something or someone from his past.

"Son, I've been through some rough patches and I always came out the other side a better man."

"Easier said than done," Bud said glumly. Would his rampaging demons allow that to happen?

"Oh God, yes! But I think Jo sees the potential in you. That's what's drawing her close."

Golden gave Bud one of his signature winks. Then he shook his employee's hand and dashed off with a "gotta go."

After one flight of stairs, he paused.

"Good luck moving your furniture!" he yelled.

Bud heard him laughing the rest of the way down.

———

Most of his first paycheck was spent on a bed. The rest of his furnishings he got for free.

It was amazing what people threw out. What he couldn't get on Craigslist, he found on the sidewalks of Astoria's finest neighborhoods.

With his newfound skills, there wasn't a scratch, dent or hole he feared.

His biggest score was a handsome black-leather sofa that he spotted outside a palatial gingerbread Victorian on trash day. There was a small tear on the back he could patch and hide against a wall.

The trick would be getting it to his apartment. He still didn't have a vehicle.

As he stood on the curb guarding the discarded sofa and fretting that the garbage men would arrive at any moment, he saw a landscaping truck up the block.

"Didn't know you guys were still working in February," Bud said, hurrying over.

"It's slow now, but people are already booking jobs for spring," explained Bob Smart, owner of Be Smart Landscaping Co.

Admiring the trailer attached to Smart's pickup, Bud said, "Hey, any chance you can do me a small favor? I need to move that sofa over there to my place. It's just down the hill – two blocks."

Smart shook his head.

"I'll give you twenty bucks," Bud said. "That's all I have. Please?"

"Sorry, pal," the man said, opening the driver's door. "I'm not a mover."

"Valentine's Day is next week, boss. If I don't get that sofa in my apartment, my girl is gonna leave me."

The man groaned.

Moments later, they were parked in front of The Royal, pulling the sofa out of the trailer.

"Give me that twenty," Smart demanded.

"Sure," Bud said. "Soon as we get it upstairs."

9

Robbie had seen a lot of stuff go down in the Safeway parking lot. Stoners firing up bongs. Couples having sex in back seats, steaming up windows. Even a mugging and a rampaging pit bull.

But in all his months herding shopping carts, the Astoria High School senior never saw a customer freeze outside the glass front doors.

And yet, there the dude was, cemented to the ground like a friggin' statue.

As curious customers filed by, doing their best not to stare, Robbie sprang into action. He had to. How else was he going to get his train of stacked carts inside the store?

The 17-year-old with braces approached the man gingerly and saw he was in some kind of daze, breathing super-fast. His hands were shaking and his forehead was moist with sweat.

"Dude, you okay?"

Robbie tapped him on the shoulder.

"Mister?"

Bud didn't hear or see the teenager. He was lost, trapped in a warped, furious flashback that had dragged him down to some unknown place.

In his mind, he was holding a sack of stolen money in each hand.

The security guard is coming. The Wells Fargo truck is pulling up.

Scratching his downy goatee, Robbie pondered the situation, drawing on his best video game problem-solving skills. Maybe the dude was having a stroke. Maybe he should call an ambulance.

He could try moving him to the side, he supposed, but what if that made him freak out even more?

As a small crowd of shoppers began to gather, the cart wrangler settled on a solution: He'd tell the manager.

Robbie ran off as the stranger shut his eyes and doubled over in pain. The manager, bespectacled and wearing a gold vest with a nametag pinned to it, arrived at the scene in less than a minute.

He approached the man – now leaning against a wall, struggling to catch his breath – carefully, like a soldier crossing a minefield.

"Sir, can I help you?"

With Robbie's help, the manager tried moving the man to a bench by the entrance.

The security guard grabs him. The robber swings his arm to break free and …

The manager fell to the ground.

"Oh fuck, the dude hit Bob!" Robbie yelled. "Somebody call the cops!"

Two of Astoria's finest responded quickly. Bud was leaning against the wall, trembling. The manager was sitting on the ground, nursing a sore jaw.

The cops took one look at Bud with his odd, vacant expression and nodded at each other. Another strung-out junkie.

"This guy's out of it," one of the officers said. "Cuff him. We'll take him to Columbia Memorial for an eval."

They put him in the back of their black cruiser. At the hospital, the ER doctor examined Bud, who was no longer incapacitated but still breathing hard.

"He's not high," he told the officers afterward. "He's having some kind of stress-related episode. I'll give him something to relax him. He should be fine in a couple of hours."

The cops took Bud to the local jail and had him booked on a simple assault charge.

His haze lifted when the sedatives kicked in. He found himself lying on a cot in a cell with cinderblock walls, a stainless-steel toilet and a concrete floor.

Thinking he was back in the Idaho prison, he screamed in horror.

"Help! Help!"

The jailer came with a Taser in his hand. Bud was squeezing the bars in the door with all his strength.

"Where am I? What the fuck am I doing here?"

Experienced with strange outbursts by his incarcerated guests, the burly man grumbled: "You're in the Clatsop County Jail. Now just relax. Scream again and I'll zap you."

"What did I do?"

"You punched someone," the man said, shaking his head. He was also used to blacked-out drunks waking up in his facility.

"*What?*"

"Sit down and shut up."

Bud paced the tiny cell in circles, trying to remember. His last clear memory was walking through downtown. He was going to buy some food staples for his kitchen.

Questions flooded his brain: Who did he punch? How badly was he hurt? Where did this happen and why?

The jailer reappeared a short time later, this time with a ring of keys. He opened the cell door and walked away.

A woman in a pink coat was standing there.

"Hey Bud."

"Jo Jo?"

Bud moved closer and could see her face, clouded with concern.

"Why are you here?" he asked. "How did you—"

"I was here when they brought you in, but you didn't recognize me."

"What the hell happened?"

"You were outside a supermarket and had some kind of nervous breakdown. You hit the manager when he tried to help you."

"Good Lord, I don't remember any of that."

"The good news is you're free to go. I'm supposed to keep an eye on you, make sure you take your meds."

Jo Jo shook the yellow pill bottle in her hand.

"Come on, let's get out of here."

———

They ended up at Bud's pier, just before sunset. His whiskered friends had found another gathering place for the night.

For a while, the only sound was water gently splashing against the rocks.

Finally, she turned to him and asked, "What aren't you telling me?"

He felt his gut tighten. She deserved to know about his past but telling her would likely mean he'd never see her again.

"I think I had a flashback. I was in the middle of it when I hit that man."

"What kind of flashback? About what?"

After another long pause, Bud looked into her lovely face and said, "I've done some bad things."

"You've been in prison, haven't you?" Jo Jo said, startling Bud.

"How did you know?"

"I work with prisoners, get inside their heads. I think I knew from the moment I first saw you, whistling on this pier. I knew from some of the things you said, like the way you call Harry 'boss.'"

Bud hung his head.

"How long were you in prison?"

"Twenty-five years," he said, watching Jo Jo's eyes widen. He'd lost her now for sure.

"I thought I'd never get out, but one night they put me on a bus, and here I am. I became something of a jailhouse lawyer. I sued the prison system, forced them to make changes to fix some serious problems. I was a huge pain in the ass."

Jo Jo studied Bud for a while.

"What bad things did you do?"

"I robbed supermarkets. I was a foolish kid, in my twenties, never thought I'd get caught. I'd blow the money on booze and babes, and then do it again."

He quickly added: "I scared a lot of people, put guns in their faces, but I never hurt anyone – I *swear*."

"Well, that explains your breakdown outside the Safeway. Oh, Bud."

She stood and brushed herself off.

"It's getting dark," she said. "I need to take you to your apartment. You're technically on house arrest."

When they made it up the stairs at The Royal, he expected her to say goodbye. For good.

Instead, she followed him inside.

Looking around, Jo Jo was astonished by the transformation. She could smell the fresh paint and varnish.

"Oh my gosh, you did all this?"

Bud was relieved.

"I'm glad you like it."

She leafed through his stack of do-it-yourself books, admired his shining floors.

"You really did this all yourself? Wow. It may be the best apartment in town."

"The best *free* apartment, for sure."

"I think I underestimated you. I kinda thought you'd cut and run, no offense."

"Those thoughts did enter my mind from time to time. Of course, I had an ulterior motive."

"Oh yeah?"

"I wanted you to visit, and I know you wouldn't hang out in a dump. You're too classy for that."

"Classy with a 'k.' I work at the jail and a homeless shelter, Bud."

"I don't mean classy like you're a snob. I mean sophisticated, with good taste."

"Well, I do love this," she said, running her hand over the leather sofa.

Jo Jo dropped her shoulder bag on one of the overstuffed cushions and asked, "May I use your refurbished bathroom?"

"You may," Bud said with an exaggerated bow.

The bathroom door closed and Bud plopped onto the sofa. Looking out the windows, he could see a row of freighters awaiting cargo anchored in the river. The barks of the sea lions, wherever they were, penetrated the walls.

Leaning back, he noticed Jo Jo's bag was open. He could see her wallet inside.

Bud opened the bag a little wider with the touch of a finger. The red wallet bulged, begging to be touched.

He found himself licking his lips in anticipation. The wallet was pulsing now, like a beating heart.

His hand, seemingly moving on its own accord, floated over the bag.

Regaining his senses, Bud yanked it back.

Oh my God, what am I doing? What's wrong with me?

There was a flushing sound, followed by running water. Bud jumped to his feet seconds before Jo Jo returned.

"Are you okay? You look a little pale."

"Just tired."

"You should rest. You've had quite a day."

She reached in her bag, fished out the pill bottle and tossed it to Bud.

"Don't forget to take those until you feel like yourself."

At the front door, she turned to face him.

"You've been given a rare gift, Bud," she said, sounding like Jenkins, the State Police commander.

"A second chance."

10

"Sully! Call for you!"

The bowtied owner of Frontier Ridge General Store popped up like a whack-a-mole from behind the counter where he was restocking ammunition.

"What's that?"

Saul "Sully" Sullivan didn't hear so well these days.

He was 88 years old and had been around guns and dynamite all his life. He didn't see too well, either, and he walked with a limp thanks to a near-fatal encounter with a Kodiak bear when he was a young man.

He'd show you the scars if you asked. If you didn't, he'd still tell you the story about how he got them.

"Phone! Some guy named Bud asking for you!"

Sullivan shuffled over in his half-hunched way and grabbed the phone from his nephew.

"This is Sully," he said, slightly out of breath.

"Hello, I'm Bud Baker. You probably don't remember me. I'm trying to find Elmore. He's not answering his phone."

The shopkeeper shook his head sadly. "Son, Elmore's not going to be taking any calls."

"Why's that?"

"On account of he's dead. Passed away two years ago."

"Oh, sorry to hear."

There goes my sponsor.

"Yeah, we were good pals. What were you looking to talk to old Elmore about?"

"I was going to ask him about the cabin I bought from him. I've been gone a long time and just wanted to make sure it was still standing."

"Ah, I remember you now. Elmore brought you to the store, introduced you all around. Young feller with bushy hair."

"That's right."

"Yeah, Elmore's old place is still there, probably will be for another 100 years."

"Well, that's a relief."

"Elmore had it boarded up after he got sick, said you'd be coming back to live there some day."

"That's the plan. Just got delayed is all."

"I'll say. Stop by here on your way up, and I'll give you the keys and set you up with some provisions," Sullivan said.

"Thanks, I'll be there after the thaw. Sorry again about your friend."

Bud hung up and stepped out of one of Astoria's last public phone booths, sandwiched between a gas station and a salmon smokehouse. He now had a few hundred dollars in a bank account but still couldn't afford one of those touchscreen smart phones that seemed to be everywhere.

He also didn't have a watch, which sometimes made him either very early or very late for whatever he had to do.

Bud looked up at the sky and frowned. A thick layer of clouds prevented him from seeing the position of the sun, like a sailor. He picked up his pace, headed for the church.

When he got to First Christian, the clothing drive he'd volunteered for was well underway. Jo Jo was there, sorting through donations as Bud ambled over with a big smile.

"Hello, Bud," she said, a bit sadly. Not bothering to make eye contact, she kept sorting, tossing out any garments with tears, holes or permanent stains.

Bud joined in, standing beside her.

"You okay?"

He hadn't seen Jo Jo for a few weeks. She'd lost weight, looking slightly gaunt. There were bags under her eyes.

"Sure," she said, unconvincingly. "How's the apartment-managing going?"

"Not too bad," Bud said, eyeballing a flannel shirt and judging it worthy. "Old Miss Caruthers in No. 2 is always calling with something. I think she wants me."

"I see."

"She's 75. That was a joke."

"Sorry, I'm not very fun these days. You really don't want to be around me."

"Hey, no problem. We all have our bad days. I'm practically an expert. I've had some bad *years*."

They worked in silence for a while, discarding, sorting and folding until the big pile in front of them was gone.

Bud watched Jo Jo's face and even though he barely knew her, he could tell something was seriously wrong.

"Hey, let me buy you a drink. I want to hear what's making you so sad."

"No, you don't. But thanks."

"Just a drink. What's the harm in that?"

She looked deeply into Bud's brown eyes, saw the safe harbor inside.

"Okay, Bud. One drink."

Bud smiled and Jo Jo couldn't help but do the same.

They walked down the hill to a cannery-turned-brewery that extended out over the water. The popular establishment had a few glass panels in the floor near the bar, allowing customers to watch critters swim by, but the best feature was the stunning view of the river from its many big windows. Also, the beer was tasty.

They sat at a table for two, sipped their IPAs and snacked on fried cheese curds with a tangy dipping sauce.

"You're a beautiful woman, Jo Jo," he blurted.

She blushed, a small explosion of pink against her snowy skin. "Yeah, right."

"Even when you're depressed. That's amazing."

"And you've cleaned up nicely, sir."

He was wearing form-fitting jeans, deck shoes and a woolly fisherman's sweater. His beard was neatly trimmed, the mop of curls tamed just right. He was more fit than before, thanks largely to those three flights of stairs to his apartment.

Jo Jo suddenly found herself attracted to a man who used to rob people for a living. It wasn't unusual for female social workers to fall for charming cons, but, despite all her work with prisoners, that had never happened to her.

Now she struggled to resist her feelings for the man seated across from her. The reformed felon who'd been responsible for a one-man crime wave.

After a second beer, Jo Jo began to relax and feel more like herself. She laughed at his dumb jokes and pointed out the bobbing head of a sea lion in the water, watching with a smile as he jumped up to take a look.

"There's something about you, Bud. Something peaceful."

"Funny, I was just thinking something similar."

"Oh yeah? What?"

"How calming you are, like ocean surf."

"You haven't heard my story yet. The story that makes me so sad. You've opened up to me about your past, and I haven't returned the favor."

"I'd like to hear it. That's why we're here, right?"

They ordered a third round as Jo Jo silently debated whether it would be best to leave now and never talk to this man again – wall him off from her fractured life. Keep her miseries under lock and key.

But Bud put his elbows on the table, rested his chin on his hands and waited, with those trusting puppy eyes.

"I had a client who was an addict – heroin mostly," she began, speaking softly so only the two of them could hear. "She did whatever she could to get to the next high – stealing, sex with strangers. The usual.

"She got pregnant and went to rehab. Despite everything she'd been through, she really, really wanted that baby. She bought a crib and diapers, the whole thing. She was clean all the way through the pregnancy and then, days before the baby was due, the man she was sleeping with became insanely jealous and tried to kill the fetus by injecting her with a mix of heroin and fentanyl."

"How'd he do that?"

"He ground up a sleeping pill and put it in her orange juice, and when she was knocked out he put a needle in her arm. But the woman began overdosing violently. So rather than risk a murder rap, this man put her in his car and dropped her off at the ER. Actually, he dumped her on the sidewalk outside the entrance and took off."

"Holy cow."

"There's more. When she came to, she was lying in a bed in the maternity ward, but her belly was empty. Her baby was gone. She screamed, and a nurse came and told her the baby had died. The drugs in her had killed it. When she made it home that night she was devastated. She attempted suicide and nearly succeeded."

Bud couldn't believe what he was hearing.

"Jesus, Jo——" he began, but she put up a hand to stop him.

"It gets stranger. What the woman was told was a lie. The baby didn't die at birth. The baby was perfectly healthy – healthy enough to be adopted by a couple here in Astoria."

Bud's jaw dropped.

"What do you think of my story so far?" Jo Jo said, taking a gulp of beer.

The ex-convict's legal brain was churning. "So, the birth mother has no idea her baby is alive?"

"She does now. Because I told her."

Bud's brow furrowed.

"I'm sorry, I must be missing something."

"The nurse in the maternity ward falsified records, saying the baby boy was stillborn. In reality, she swaddled the infant and hid him until her shift ended. Then she delivered the baby to an adoption agency in town, Little Angels."

"I'm starting to get the picture."

"It's a black-market operation, Bud. This may sound crazy, but I think they're selling stolen babies."

"How do you know any of this?"

"The nurse who lied, Anna Kendrall is her name, quit a few days later. I had been at the hospital demanding answers and she got my number. She told me to come see her, that she couldn't talk on the phone, so I did. She told me what happened – her part, anyway. It was like a confession, tears and all. She said she was paid five grand.

"When I went back later to try to convince her to go to police or give a sworn statement, she was gone. Her apartment was cleared out. The landlord had no idea where she went."

"Did you go to the adoption agency?"

"I did, but they told me the nurse had been fired and her story was a big lie, and if I went around asking any more questions, they'd sue me for slander."

There were tears in her eyes.

"It's so … so terrible."

"You need to go to the police," Bud said, trying to be helpful. "You have contacts there. They'll take you seriously. They'll do an investigation and the bad people will be arrested, and a judge will order the baby be returned to its mother."

Jo Jo shook her head sadly.

"We can't go to the police. The chief of detectives is on the adoption agency board, along with other city leaders. They won't open an investigation."

"How do you know until you try?"

She looked away.

"I did. The chief of detectives was my fiancé."

Bud exhaled loudly. "The plot thickens."

"I begged him to look into it and he finally agreed. I think he just wanted me to stop talking about it. A couple weeks later, he told me he had investigated – interviewed everyone – and found no evidence of any laws being broken."

"What about the nurse?"

"He said he tracked her down in Texas and she recanted everything. She made it all up to make the hospital look bad, he said."

"Damn."

"I broke up with him the next day. I couldn't marry someone who'd lie to my face. I know what the nurse told me was true."

"I'm sorry. How long ago was that?"

"Five and a half months."

She looked at Bud, saw his deep concern.

"I know where the baby is, where the adoptive parents live," she said.

"So, you can go there, talk to them?"

Jo Jo shook her head.

"Would you just hand over a beautiful baby boy, five months later?"

"Maybe, if they knew he was stolen. How could they live with what they did to the birth mother?"

"They don't know that part."

"Tell them, see what happens."

"It won't work," she said, shaking her head. "They won't believe me."

Bud pondered the story for a while then looked at Jo Jo closely.

"It's all very tragic. I'm sorry."

"Strangely, I feel better. I guess I had to tell someone, get it out. You're a better listener than I thought you'd be."

He laughed.

"Maybe one of these days you'll stop underestimating me."

11

Weeks passed before Jo Jo agreed to a date with Bud — lattés and a shared apple-cinnamon muffin at Coffee Girl.

The small, friendly café was located inside yet another former cannery on a pier that sliced far enough into the river that people drove over it to get there.

When their fingertips touched accidentally over the plate, Jo Jo's face flushed. Bud felt the same spark.

"No, you have the last bite," he said in his most gentlemanly manner.

She had turned his invitations down twice but finally relented after she spotted him feeding feral cats in the bushes behind The Royal. The shield around her heart melted.

Jo Jo watched him from around the corner and knew it was an act of kindness he'd keep to himself, like how he'd stop in at the shelter to talk to the homeless men, giving them the respect they craved.

The ex-con and the social worker, it turned out, weren't such a mismatch after all. He was 11 years older, but she didn't have a problem with that.

After dating for a while, Jo Jo found that she respected Bud's inner strength and kind heart, hidden from most people under layers of sandpaper-like toughness. She enjoyed his stories and instinctively knew when he was melancholy and needed space.

Bud felt from the start that he was under Jo Jo's spell. Everything she did seemed magical, from the way her eyes shined when she laughed to how she brushed her long, silky hair.

She was the smartest person Bud had ever known and he enjoyed her rapier wit immensely. But it was her patience he came to admire most.

The first time they made love, Bud was a nervous wreck and couldn't perform.

Jo Jo knew just what to say and do to soothe his fragile male ego. They cuddled in bed as candles flickered and soft music played.

After a while, he reached over and began tenderly tracing circles on her lower back with his fingers.

He slowly kissed her firm breasts, sucking each pink nipple in turn. By the time he tongued her belly button, she was moaning with anticipation.

Bud put his head between her legs and she guided him to the right spot, grasping his curly hair with both hands.

Minutes later, he entered her – slowly at first, inch by inch. She shuddered and arched her back, inviting him to go deeper.

Rising to his knees, he began rocking, faster and faster. With a final thrust, she screamed in pleasure as he came inside her.

"Oh my God," Bud whispered as they collapsed in each other's arms. "Did you like it?"

"Get some rest, buster," she said, running her fingers through the hair on his still-heaving chest. "I'm not done with you yet."

During their romantic early dates, Jo Jo made sure Bud didn't exhaust his meager savings on expensive dinners and nights out. It wouldn't have impressed her anyway – material things were not the key to her heart. Instead, she insisted on picking up the tab every other time – and firmly but lovingly enforced the relationship rule.

She also helped him put the finishing decorative touches on his apartment and began leaving some of her clothes and makeup there. They had become a couple, but she didn't give up her own place – she needed a refuge of her own.

He regaled her with tales of his life as an outlaw and a convict, and the many strange characters he encountered. One day, when she questioned the veracity of one of his accounts, he got up and disappeared in the bedroom closet.

She heard him moving boxes around. He returned with a triumphant look on his face.

The newspaper with his profile in it was in his hands. Bobbie G. mailed it to him after Bud sent his former cellmate a postcard from Astoria to apologize for not saying goodbye.

Jo Jo read the story in amazement.

"Oh my God, it's true. All of it."

———

Bud was sitting on his sofa smoking a joint and listening to classic Bob Marley tunes when someone knocked.

He opened the door and was surprised to see Jo Jo. They weren't planning to get together that evening.

She had a bottle of wine in her hand and an intoxicating smile.

"The supermarket manager dropped the assault charge. You're a free man – again. Can I come in?"

"Well, I don't know," Bud said playfully. "I'm kinda busy."

Jo Jo brushed by him and took a sniff.

"The party has already started, I see."

She walked over to the ashtray on the coffee table and took a hit off the joint. She coughed and burst out laughing.

"Last time I did that was college."

Bud uncorked the cabernet sauvignon and poured a couple of glasses. He had acquired a TV set – for free, naturally – and they sipped their wine and watched a sitcom for a while.

Bud spun the bottle and saw it was from a winery in the Sonoma Valley region of California.

"I did a robbery there, in Santa Rosa. Back when I was posing as an armored car guard."

"Why didn't you just run inside, wave a gun and grab cash from the registers?"

"The real money is in the safe. Besides, there was this sort of Butch Cassidy vibe to it. I found it thrilling."

"How much money did you get away with? I mean, in total. That wasn't in the profile."

Bud laughed. "A lot. Maybe a million."

"Holy cow!"

"Yeah, but I wasted it all. The only useful thing I ever bought was a log cabin outside of Kodiak, Alaska."

"That's where you want to go settle down, isn't it? Why there and not, oh, I don't know, some island in the Caribbean where it doesn't snow?"

"My dad took me to Kodiak in the summer when I was a boy. There was a small lake there, up in the hills. That's where the cabin is. It's paradise, or at least it seemed like it at the time."

He gazed into Jo Jo's ever-changing mermaid eyes, now a mix of green and gold.

"I was hoping you'd go there with me. It's boarded up now, but with your help, it could be homey. Logs crackling in the fireplace, bearskin rug ..."

"From an actual bear?"

"You'd like it."

"The bear won't, I bet."

Bud rolled his eyes and Jo Jo gave him a little shove.

"It does sound like paradise," she said.

"In the summer, when the bald eagles are soaring and the sockeye are jumping, there's no better place."

"But in the winter, brrr."

"*In the winter* ... have you ever seen the Northern Lights?"

"You mean the aurora borealis? I've seen pictures in magazines."

"Pictures don't do it justice. In Alaska, on those long winter nights, when the skies are especially dark and the air is just frigid enough, that's when the magic happens."

Just talking about it put some sparkle in his eyes. He became a boy describing his favorite toy.

"Imagine shimmering curtains of green light, laced with a delicate purple, dancing over your head," he said, hands waving like a wizard casting a spell.

"Ooh, sounds beautiful."

"Beautiful. Mystical. Spiritual? Some people love fireworks. I love the Northern Lights. I only saw it once in person, when I was passing through Fairbanks as a young man. I looked up and there were these glowing whirlpools in the sky. It took my breath away.

"The locals said it had something to do with sunspots and space magnetism and stuff, but I could tell they were just as blown away as I was. I think it's as close to a religious experience as I've ever had. I can't wait to see it again."

He looked deeply into Jo Jo's eyes.

"I want *you* to see it," he said.

She kissed his cheek.

"I love it when you get excited about something. You're more complex than the average convict."

"Ex-convict, if you please."

They drank more wine and finished the joint. She got up to look out the living room window at the water. When she turned around the expression on her face was one he hadn't seen before.

There was a fierceness to it.

"Bud, there's something about my story with the baby I didn't tell you."

"What's that?"

"I didn't tell you the whole truth. That woman wasn't really my client."

Bud had a gut feeling that was the case.

"Her name is Jessie. She's 35 years old. The baby was the reason she cleaned herself up, got a job, fixed up her apartment. That child was going to be the foundation of the new life she was building, her guiding star. I'm afraid for her now. I'm afraid of what she might do."

Jo Jo gazed into Bud's eyes, trying to gauge his feelings.

"Jessie is my sister," she said.

"What?"

"Our parents died in a car crash years ago. I'm all she has. I have to help her."

She slumped on the couch and Bud gave her a hug.

"Why didn't you tell me?"

"I should have. You told me the truth about your past, now I'm doing the same. I moved here because of Jessie. I became a social worker because of her. I was desperate to help her, to save her. I still am.

"I wasn't at the hospital the night they took her baby, Bud. I promised Jessie I'd be at her side in the delivery room when the time came, and I … failed her."

Tears rolled down Jo Jo's cheek and Bud brushed them away.

"There was nothing you could do. You didn't know."

"They even robbed us of a proper funeral," she said. "They said Jessie requested cremation, but she doesn't remember doing that. They offered us ashes – from somebody or some thing, I suppose – not a body. She and I did a small memorial service on the riverbank a couple days later. The nurse called the next day, and I learned the truth about those grotesque liars."

Bud struggled to process the new information. He loved Jo Jo, more than any woman in his life. His instinct was to help her in any way he could.

And then, as if reading his mind, she made a staggering request.

"We have to do something for Jessie. Something dangerous."

Bud recoiled.

"*Dangerous?*"

"Darling," she said, "I need you to steal that baby."

12

Astoria was in the sweet embrace of spring.

A promising warmth filled the breeze blowing off the pier as Bud sat on the edge. The air was perfumed with the season's first flowers.

Up north, on a Kodiak hilltop, the snow would be melting, clearing the way for his return. He hoped Jo Jo would be joining him, but that seemed unlikely now.

It had been a week since he last saw her.

He loved her, but he couldn't do what she asked. He couldn't revert to his criminal ways and kidnap someone's baby.

That terrible night, she sobbed and he yelled. He hadn't seen her since.

Steal a baby?

He'd do almost anything for Jo Jo, but *that*? Why would she even ask him to risk being thrown back in a prison cell for the rest of his life?

Bud was still struggling with flashbacks. The war between his demons and angels was far from over. He'd only recently been able to step inside a grocery store.

What would happen to his battered psyche if he repeated some of the worst things he'd ever done?

Bud questioned whether his romance with Jo Jo had been a set-up – a con of an ex-con. Maybe she only wanted a felon with experience tying up and robbing people to come along and do her a favor.

Is our love a big lie?

No, he wouldn't steal a baby. No fucking way.

He pulled a pint of whiskey from his coat and took a swig.

Good day to get drunk.

"Can I have some of that?"

He looked up, startled, as Jo Jo sat next to him, sighing heavily.

Bud handed her the bottle and she took a drink.

"Thanks."

He turned his gaze back to the Columbia's blue waters. There were a million things he wanted to tell her, but he couldn't speak.

That was how relationships died, he supposed. The loving words went unspoken for too long.

"I don't want to lose you," she said.

Bud listened, saying nothing.

"I'm so sorry," she continued. "I wasn't thinking. It was too much to ask. Far too much."

"I feel bad for her, I really do," he said. "I just can't risk going back to prison. Kidnap a baby from some rich white people? They'll hang me."

"I know. It was wrong of me to ask."

They sat for a while in sadness, watching the seagulls soar.

"I miss you," she said.

Bud felt a longing in his heart. Since meeting Jo Jo, all his defenses had fallen.

"I miss you, too. I'm really sorry about Jessie."

"You were right, though. I just have to deal with it. I mean, in some ways she's doing better than I am, to tell the truth."

After a long moment of river-gazing, Jo Jo said, "I want you to meet her. She's planning to leave, make a fresh start in Nevada – get away from the dealers and the junkies she knows here. Too much temptation."

"That's smart. Are you going with her?"

Bud dreaded what her answer might be, but he had to know.

"She doesn't want me to, says she needs to do this on her own. Called me her 'crutch.' But I'll worry, of course."

"I'd love to meet her. Is she a smoking hot ginger like you?"

"That's enough out of you," she said. "I'll set something up."

———

The house where Jessie lived was almost directly under Astoria Bridge, the miles-long span of steel and asphalt rising high enough over the Columbia to let the ocean-going freighters pass.

Bud could hear the steady thunder of cars and trucks rolling across the bridge binding Oregon to Washington.

Jessie's apartment was on the first floor of an oversized 1925 Craftsman off the river that probably once housed a sea captain and his family. It was now a boarding house, carved into a half-dozen units.

The home's century-old elegance was long gone, at least on the outside.

Several windows were boarded up. The yard, such as it was, was filled with trash, including a rusted bicycle and dented washing machine. The front porch was rotting. Paint was peeling off the siding.

"Nice place," Bud teased as Jo Jo guided him around to a rear entrance.

"It's not so bad inside. You'll see."

Jo Jo had her own key and let herself in after a couple of quick knocks.

Bud didn't know what to expect of Jessie.

He had been around addicts before and it wasn't a pretty sight. Especially the heroin junkies. They often no longer cared about their physical appearance, only the next high. Some resembled zombies, with their sunken eyes and tremors, always just one injection away from a possible fatal overdose.

But Jessie welcomed her visitors with a warm smile. She was attractive like her sister, but a couple of inches shorter, with shoulder-length blonde hair and caramel eyes.

"Coffee?"

"Not for me," Jo Jo said.

"I'm good," Bud answered.

They sat in a square living room that was tastefully decorated with pre-owned but elegant furniture, a braided rug and old movie posters.

"So, you're Bud," she said, smiling. "I've heard a lot about you."

"Hopefully only good things," he said. It was a joke, but he really preferred not to go through the whole 25-years-in-prison thing.

"JJ tells me you renovated your apartment and it's wonderful."

Bud chuckled. "Lots of mistakes, but it turned out okay. I like this place, with the high ceilings and built-ins. But I hear you're moving?"

The sisters exchanged glances.

"It's time," Jessie said. "I need to start fresh somewhere."

Jo Jo patted her kid sister's leg. "She's become a foodie. She wants to maybe open a small restaurant, right Jess?"

"One of these days. Right now, I'm waitressing part-time and can barely pay the rent."

"Well, at least you're in the restaurant biz," Bud said, trying to sound encouraging.

They chatted for a while about her plans to move to the Las Vegas area and start over in a drier place, free of the Pacific Northwest's constant dampness.

Jessie was the one who brought up her struggles with drugs.

Surprisingly candid, she spoke of how, like most addicts, she started out thinking she could shoot heroin on a recreational basis and maintain her life – achieve some measure of equilibrium. She'd go to work, get high afterward, then repeat the cycle.

But the drug, at least for her, wouldn't be controlled. Soon, she'd have to try making it through a shift while under its influence. Not long after that, she didn't bother going to work. She was in a full downward spiral.

When she woke after tripping all night, the first thing she'd think about was shooting up again, she told Bud.

"JJ saved me. She had a life in California, but she just picked up and moved here. She got me into rehab."

"You saved yourself," the big sister said. "You just needed a push."

Jessie took a sip of her coffee and looked at Bud.

"I suppose she's told you about the baby," she said.

"Yeah, I'm so sorry."

"As a mother, that's something you can never put aside: the loss of a child. That kind of hurt runs too deep, doesn't it?"

Bud was about to try to answer when Jessie went on.

"I always wanted to be a mother. Getting married? Not so much. I just wanted to be a mom. I'm a nurturer by nature. So, when I returned home from the hospital empty-handed, well … it was rough. I had been looking forward to that moment for a long time. And suddenly, it was taken away."

She dabbed her moist eyes with a tissue.

"I regret the drugs, the people I fell in with. Looking back, I'm sure I'd have my baby now if it wasn't for my past rising up to punish me."

"You can't blame yourself," Jessie said gently. "You did nothing wrong. They stole your child."

"Don't worry, sis. I'm moving on, literally."

They made some meatloaf sandwiches and went outside to enjoy the sunny day. There was a wide bench facing the river and they sat there – three in a row – trying to ignore the aggressive seagulls squawking and begging for crumbs.

Bud told some of the raunchy jokes he learned behind bars and made the women chuckle.

"So, you'll be heading to Alaska soon?" Jessie asked him.

"Still saving up, but yeah, I hope so." He looked at Jo Jo, who still hadn't committed to going with him.

Jessie, like all little sisters, pushed her sibling.

"What about it, sis? Alaska?"

Jo Jo shrugged in a playful way.

"He hasn't really asked me. Just hinted around the edges."

Bud groaned. "I didn't know you needed an engraved invitation."

He got down on his knees, theatrically.

"Josephine, dearest, would you please, please, *please* go with me to Kodiak Island?"

"I'll think about it," she said, and they all laughed.

————

Jo Jo and her sister had lived a normal life – until it wasn't.

Their father was a chemist for a pharmaceutical firm, their mother a high school English teacher. The family lived in the Oakland hills in a nice, but not luxurious, ranch-style home.

It was just assumed that Josephine would go to college and she did, majoring in international studies at UC Berkeley with visions of working at either the United Nations or the State Department as part of a diplomatic mission.

Jessie's pursuits were more physical. She parlayed her prowess as a high school soccer star into a full scholarship at USC.

But neither of them realized their dreams, because one terrible night both of their parents died.

Sam and Claire Summers were headed home from a dinner party. They were on a narrow, fog-shrouded road that snaked up a wooded hill when a deer suddenly jumped in front of their car, and Sam swerved to avoid hitting it.

Their Honda Accord smashed through a guardrail and plunged down an embankment, rolling several times and bursting into flames. They both died instantly.

Jo Jo, 23, was home listening to music when the policeman knocked on the door. Jessie, 18, was at the park, practicing her soccer moves. In a flash, their lives were transformed.

After the funeral, Jo Jo dropped out of grad school to help her younger sister. She put her plans on hold.

Jessie, meanwhile, became sullen and withdrawn. She stopped practicing and surrendered her scholarship.

The more Jo Jo fretted over her sibling's depression, the more Jessie rebelled – until one day she packed her bags and announced she was moving north, to Astoria. She had a girlfriend there and needed a break, she said.

Partly to cope with her own emotional wounds, Jo Jo pivoted and became a social worker. By day, she'd counsel criminals and help the homeless. Every night she called her sister, who reassured her she was doing fine.

After a few months, Jo Jo's calls starting going unanswered for days at a time. When Jessie did pick up the phone, she didn't sound right.

Worried, the big sister drove to Oregon to see what was going on. She was stunned by what she saw.

Jessie was living in a flophouse where people were lying around smoking crack and shooting up. While she denied she was using drugs herself, Jo Jo knew better.

On her next visit to Astoria, Jo Jo found her sister passed out on the floor. She got her to a hospital, where the doctor said she had overdosed on heroin.

That night, Jo Jo made arrangements to move to the city and get Jessie in rehab. There would be several relapses and more treatment, but eventually, with Jo Jo's patient nurturing, Jessie kicked the habit.

She began taking care of herself, exercising again and working. She started thinking about her future for the first time in years. Maybe she'd save up and open a cute little café, she told her sister.

Then she got pregnant and everything changed – again.

13

For a while, Jo Jo seemed happy.

She and Bud had fallen in love – a thrilling enchantment that made their life together seem so wonderful. So perfect. So limitless.

But then Bud would catch Jo Jo in tears at odd times and in odd places – sometimes in the bathroom staring blankly in the mirror or wandering aimlessly along the waterfront – and he knew her sadness had returned.

He blamed himself for her descents into darkness at first, as if he alone was responsible. But, gradually, he came to realize that the true source of her gloom was a lost baby.

The older sister, the self-declared protector, had failed.

"I told you I'm bad news," Jo Jo would say, wiping away a tear. But Bud would squeeze her tight and her mood would brighten – if only for a few hours.

Just as he was starting to lose hope, an idea popped in his head. He walked into the living room where Jo Jo was reading a paperback novel and gently pulled it from her hands.

"There's something we can do," he said. "A way to fight back."

"What are you talking about?"

"I'm talking about Jessie and the baby. I don't know why I didn't think of this before, but we need to write up everything we know about this scheme and what happened to her. Your talk with the nurse, with Little Angels, the chief of detectives – every single detail."

Jo Jo sat up straight. "And do what?"

"I was a jailhouse lawyer, right? I know how to write a compelling argument based on facts. So, we write it up and mail it to the FBI and investigative reporters."

Bud's enthusiasm was beginning to rub off on Jo Jo, but she had some doubts.

"What if Little Angels sues me for slander or whatever?"

"Baby, the truth is our defense. Besides, we don't need to put our names to it. We'll sign it 'Anonymous.'"

Jo Jo thought for a minute and then smiled in an unburdened way that Bud hadn't seen for many days.

"I love it! When can we start?"

Bud dropped a legal pad on the coffee table.

"Way ahead of you."

They spent the rest of the night working on the statement, with Jo Jo dictating the details chronologically and Bud jotting them down. Then he borrowed her laptop and began to write, methodically making his case just like he had a dozen times behind bars.

The next day, Bud showed his girlfriend a five-page draft. She read it closely and gave him a big kiss.

"It might work," she said brightly.

"It just might."

The missive attempted to explain why Jessie's rights were violated when the baby was taken from her at the hospital and "sold" for profit. It alleged that local police officials refused to take action because they were part of the scheme. It ended with a demand for a full investigation.

Neither of them owned a printer, so they took the laptop to the library and printed the document for 10 cents a page. Then they stuffed envelopes addressed to the FBI's office in Portland and the investigations team at The Oregonian, the state's largest paper.

Bud hoped the feds and serious journalists would dig into his claims.

They mailed the envelopes and waited, watching for any signs of federal agents knocking on the door at Little Angels or the paper writing anything up. Bud volunteered to walk over to the adoption center every day to look for any unusual activity, while Jo Jo monitored the Oregonian's website.

The project put Jo Jo in a sunny place, but that proved to be short-lived.

After a while, when nothing happened, it dawned on the couple that their gambit had probably failed.

They were no closer to getting Jessie her baby back.

And Jo Jo's dark moods returned.

———

"I like your sister," Bud told Jo Jo one afternoon. "She has a good heart, like you."

They were driving home from a lunch out with Jessie. It was Bud's idea. He hoped that seeing her sister for the first time in two weeks would cheer Jo Jo up.

It seemed to. But by the time lunch was over and they were in the car, he could see the sadness in her eyes.

"She's better than me, in many ways," she said. "What's happened to her, it's so awful."

"It's been awful for you, too."

Jo Jo parked her red Toyota Corolla in front of The Royal but she didn't get out. She had to find the strength to go to work.

The social worker had succumbed to her blues, taking her full allotment of sick days. Every morning, she woke to the alarm, showered and got dressed in her work clothes. But when she got to the door, she couldn't turn the knob, as if repelled by some kind of force field.

That day, after lunch, Bud knew what he had to do. For Jo Jo. For her sister, too.

He kissed her velvety cheek and stepped out of the car.

"I have some thinking to do," he declared.

"About what?"

Bud smiled. "About stealing a baby from some rich white people."

Before Jo Jo could say a word, he was gone.

14

Bud was laying on his belly in tall grass.

He rolled over and saw only swirling mist. He was naked except for his boxers and his hands were covered in blood.

The ghost approached slowly, floating across the field. Bud squinted at the apparition, shielding his eyes from its unearthly glow.

"What do you want?"

The ghost was over him now and he could see a human face. A young man's face.

Bud looked down and saw a revolver in his hand. Blood was flowing now, dripping off the barrel, and he dropped the weapon in horror.

Eerie laughter crackled like lightning. Bud crawled, trying to escape, but the mist had become a dense fog. He waved his hands in front of him like a blind man.

Then he felt the body and screamed.

———

Bud woke to a piercing headache. He couldn't remember his nightmare, but he knew it was a bad one.

He took it as a warning.

For several days, he'd been thinking and acting like a criminal.

The couple who adopted Jessie's baby lived in a stately, turn-of the-century home high on a ridgetop overlooking downtown Astoria and the river. The home was set off the street, with a curving lawn and groomed shrubs, ringed by a custom wrought-iron fence.

Bud saw no evidence of an alarm system and noticed that an alley off the detached garage led to a back door that couldn't be seen by passing cars. It would be his point of entry, he decided.

He began shadowing the couple, getting to know their routines.

Like clockwork, the father, who worked as a lawyer at an office downtown, left home in his black sedan at 7:45 a.m. He returned between 5:30 and 6 p.m. The mother stayed home with the baby. She drove a minivan fitted with a child safety seat and sometimes ran errands, but usually not until the baby woke from his afternoon nap.

It pained Bud to catch glimpses of the woman tenderly holding the baby. He didn't want to hurt the parents, but, knowingly or not, they were part of a criminal scheme.

The caper, he figured, would go something like this:

He'd break into the home through the garage-side door on a Friday evening after the baby was put to bed. He'd wear a mask and gloves, and carry a small bag containing a pry bar, two pairs of handcuffs and duct tape.

At gunpoint, he'd cuff and gag the man and woman, leaving them in the basement, hidden from anyone who might approach the house the following day.

He'd carefully place the sleeping baby in a carrier and hand him off to Jessie, who would drive away, fleeing southeast to Nevada. He and Jo Jo would make a beeline north.

The biggest risk was on Jessie's part, Bud thought, since police would likely be searching for the baby by dawn the next day. But they would be looking for a man and a baby, or a couple, not a single mom.

By waiting until Friday night, Bud hoped the lawyer wouldn't be missed until Monday morning. His wife was more of a wild card. While he had observed her routine, there was no way of knowing who she regularly called or texted, and who might become alarmed if she didn't respond. He didn't believe she worked remotely because she only used a laptop occasionally, but that was also a possibility.

After several days of casing the adoptive parents, Bud called a meeting of the conspirators at his apartment.

"I have a plan," he began.

Bud went through his kidnapping plot piece by piece and the sisters, as he had insisted, said nothing until he finished.

Jo Jo and Jessie embraced afterward.

"It could work," Jo Jo told her. "You get your son back."

Jessie burst into tears, bringing the meeting to a halt for several minutes. Then the sisters began peppering Bud with questions.

"Do you have to tie up the couple?"

"Do you have to use a gun?"

Bud patiently explained that he had to handcuff the couple so they couldn't immediately call the police. His plan assumed they'd have a 24-hour head start, and they'd need every minute of that.

The revolver, he said, was just a prop, a tool. He had no intention of pulling the trigger.

"I need them to do what I say."

"What if they resist?" his girlfriend asked.

"He's a lawyer with a gut, not a Marine," Bud said. "Besides, would you resist a man in a ski mask pointing a gun at you? They'll think it's just a robbery – until it's not."

"So nobody will get hurt?" Jessie asked.

"Nobody will get hurt, I promise."

If everybody just stays cool.

"What will I do with the baby when I'm on the run? What if he cries? I'll be caught right away."

"You just have to make it to Las Vegas – a long two-day drive – but, yeah, you'll need to hide the baby somehow, keep him from making noise for a few minutes if you think you're going to be stopped."

Bud privately questioned whether a recovering addict was up to such a daunting task – fleeing police, starting over on her own. He didn't question her desire to raise a baby. He just didn't know if she could do it. Maybe she didn't either.

Those thoughts prompted him to ask Jessie a question of his own.

"How old is your baby?"

"Almost eight months, why?"

"When do they start to walk?"

"Usually around 10 months."

Bud looked relieved.

"Great! I didn't want to have to duct tape the baby."

Taking it for one of his attempts at dark humor, the women laughed nervously. Bud was really working things out in his head. He knew nothing about babies.

Jo Jo looked into Bud's eyes and saw the true danger in his plan. He was being calm so they wouldn't panic.

"And what about us?" she asked. "Alaska or bust?"

"Yeah, baby. If we do this, we can't stay here. You and your sister will be the first people they suspect.

"We'll all be fugitives," Jessie said numbly, the notion just sinking in.

"True," Bud said, "but you'll be hard to find in a busy city like Vegas. Use a different name, start over. Get rid of your car. Be a mom, like you always wanted."

He cupped Jo Jo's face in his hands.

"As for you … a cabin in the woods may not be your dream, but it's sorta off the grid."

Jo Jo said nothing. She was also processing the whole fugitive thing.

"Those documents you mailed, do you think they'll trigger anything?" Jessie asked.

"They should," Bud said. "It may just take a little time."

He hoped the claims would be dug into. If he, Jessie and Jo Jo were captured, it would be a crucial part of their defense.

While abducting a baby under normal circumstances would certainly be a serious offense, and for Bud a third strike, what if it could be proven that the baby in question had been stolen from its mother and was simply being returned?

Is it committing a crime or righting a wrong?

The meeting of the conspirators ended solemnly, with determined nods instead of high-fives. Soon, they would all be running from the law, fleeing an immediate nationwide manhunt in which every airport and transit station would be alerted.

The next day, following Bud's script, Jo Jo gave notice to her employer. She said she'd be working as a social worker in Sacramento. Jessie told her landlord she was moving to New York City.

Bud wasn't sure what to tell Golden, who had become something of a father figure, always dispensing wise advice.

Golden had been spending less and less time at The Royal as the remodeling wrapped up, turning his attention to bigger commercial projects. But Bud happened to run into him on the streets downtown.

"Just the man I was looking for," he said, slapping the businessman on the back.

"Bud! Howya doing?"

"I think I'm gonna let you make some money and rent my place out."

"You're leaving?"

"Yeah, I've got to ramble. Never meant to stay here this long, to be honest."

"Where are you headed?"

"Not sure. Someplace beautiful. Maybe Hawaii."

Golden looked at Bud wistfully.

"Well, wherever you wind up, send me a postcard. There's something special about you, my friend, and I'd like to stay in touch."

"You got it."

"And if you don't take Jo with you, you're a fool. Remember: No regrets!" That was Golden's mantra.

"No regrets," Bud repeated. "You've taught me well, old man."

"Take care of yourself. Be safe. I'm rooting for you."

The men embraced. Then Golden blessed Bud with a final wink.

15

"Jesus guides us in all we do!"

Little Angels Adoption Services clearly does the Lord's work. They say so many times in the full-color pamphlets stacked in the waiting room. But just in case anyone missed it, there was also a large painting of the Son of God hanging in the hall.

Bud sat down and smiled at the well-dressed couple holding hands across from him. He had also dressed for the occasion, visiting a barber and donning a tie and sport coat Jo Jo had picked out for him at an upscale consignment store.

He had insisted on seeing the black-market profiteers up close. He had to look them in the eye before he took them down.

As a practiced thief, he was also curious. How much were they selling babies for?

Posing as a prospective client, he made an appointment.

When he pulled open the front door at Little Angels he felt a twinge of excitement. The last time he had pretended to be someone else, he had on a gray uniform with a gun on his hip.

The agency had taken over a restored 1930s bungalow downtown, a short walk from the Clatsop County Courthouse.

The foyer was decorated with oil paintings and antiques. There was a narrow marble table with a teal porcelain vase filled with fresh-cut white roses. Classical music was playing.

Bud had never been in an adoption agency office before but this seemed more like a fancy spa.

From his seat, he could hear the man and his wife talking. The man was nervously holding a thick envelope. Bud knew instinctively it was filled with cash.

"This is how she wanted it, right?"

"Yes, honey. We do this and it's all done. We have our lovely daughter."

The man nodded and stuffed the envelope back in the breast pocket of his suit. Bud figured the couple was about to pay the "donation" for their adopted baby.

The pretend client used the bathroom and when he returned to his seat, the couple was gone.

Fifteen minutes later, the door to the director's office swung open and a smiling woman in a sky-blue business suit emerged with the parents-to-be.

"If there's anything you need, don't hesitate to call," she said cheerfully. "My number is on the card."

"We can't thank you enough," the woman said. She squeezed her husband's hand and the pair walked out with the sudden radiance of lottery winners.

"You must be George. Sorry to keep you waiting," the director said, gesturing for Bud to step inside her office. "Coffee, tea, spring water?"

"No thank you."

As Bud took a seat he saw Alison Krump slide the couple's envelope into the top drawer of her desk. In a fluid motion, she locked the drawer and settled into her antique, high-back chair.

All the while her blissful smile never faded.

"I understand you'd like some information about adoption services."

"Very much so. I apologize for my wife's absence. She has a cold and I didn't want to cancel the appointment. I know how busy you must be."

"That's kind of you. Let me tell you a little about Little Angels."

Krump was a diminutive woman in her late fifties with flat black hair trimmed in a bang above her eyebrows. Her bright red lipstick made her impossibly white teeth look even more brilliant.

She handed Bud one of the glossy pamphlets and reviewed it with the prospective client. Then she asked Bud some personal questions that he had prepared for.

After Krump suggested Bud fill out a two-page application to "start the process of creating your precious family," he surprised her by asking a direct question.

"I was wondering if you could give me a sense of what your typical, um, donation might be," he said.

The smile that had been plastered on her face tightened ever so slightly.

"We don't usually discuss that until the adoption process is further along," she said. "You understand."

Bud tried to match her smile but couldn't. His turned into a quizzical grin.

"I completely understand. I just want to be able set aside enough money. I would hate to disappoint my wife. She's been through so much."

Krump gave an empathetic nod.

"Well, we are a Christian organization, so we depend on donations from our adoptive parents. Does that help?"

Bud leaned in and lowered his voice.

"I would certainly want to match other couples' donations. My wife would insist. So, if you could give me a ballpark figure …"

"I see."

Krump wrote something on a slip of paper. She pushed it across the desk.

"This is a little unorthodox, but that should give you some idea."

Bud slid the note into his pocket without looking at it as Krump stood and escorted him to her office door.

"If there's anything you need, don't hesitate to call," she said. "I will pray for you and your wife."

"Bless you."

Jo Jo was waiting in the car when Bud appeared. Taking a seat, he pulled out the slip of paper.

His eyes widened. Written were two words: "Twenty thousand."

He showed it to Jo Jo, who blurted "Jesus!"

"Praise the Lord," he said sarcastically. "We'll have to make one more stop on the way out of town. I know where they keep the money."

"Seems risky. What if you're caught?"

"I'll be in and out in a flash."

"Are you sure?"

Bud nodded.

After meeting Krump, he knew reclaiming a baby and tipping off the feds wasn't enough.

There was no way he'd let that evil, evangelical bitch keep that money.

No goddamn way.

"Whatever those bastards made off Jessie, we're taking it back."

16

"**C**op killer!"

They formed uniformed rows and shouted at Bud as they dragged him into the jail and threw him headfirst into a holding cell, still wearing only mud-stained boxers.

Some spit on him as he passed. Some kicked. One of his eyes was already black and swollen. His upper lip was bleeding.

"Cop killer!"

"Cop killer!"

"Cop killer!"

The chants seemed to go on forever.

Bud pulled himself off the concrete floor onto the utilitarian bed. His mind reeled.

Had he fired his gun? He didn't think so.

Did he kill the deputy? No way.

All he remembered was running, trying to escape and then diving to the ground when the shooting started. His body bore the painful paths of grazing bullets.

The next morning, in his orange jumpsuit, he was hauled before a magistrate judge under heavy guard. The charges were first-degree murder and aggravated robbery with use of a deadly weapon, and prosecutors were just getting started.

He was 25 years old and his life as he knew it was over.

Bud stood before the judge, chains rattling like a Dickensian ghost, and did exactly what a man in his situation shouldn't do when asked for his plea.

He grinned like a crazy person and said, "Piss off."

————

Bud rolled out of bed, trying not to disturb Jo Jo, who was making cat-like snoring sounds. She was face-down in her pillow, strands of her scarlet hair spread out like trails of lava.

How could she sleep so soundly when their lives were about to change forever?

Tonight, we're all fugitives.

He made himself some coffee and sat alone at his breakfast table, looking through the kitchen window at the water. A massive freighter loaded with cargo containers was steaming toward the ocean. Rain clouds had parted enough to allow the sun to shine, coloring the river a deep blue.

Bud went over the plan in his head for the hundredth time, detail by detail.

At 7 p.m., he and Jo Jo would be waiting in their car, outside the house on the hill. At the same time, Jessie would be parked in a vacant industrial lot, just off Highway 30, the twisting, forested route she'd take headed east.

He and Jo Jo would watch the house, making sure the husband returned from work and the baby had been put to bed in an upstairs room, nearest the street.

Then Bud would take his bag of burglar tools and go to the side door off the garage that was shielded from the corner street light.

He'd force the lock, pull on his ski mask and take out the gun. He'd be out of the house with the baby in less than 15 minutes.

They'd then drive down the hill to Jessie's car, hand off the baby and wish her well. He and Jo Jo would continue on to the adoption agency building less than a mile away. Once he had the black-market money, they'd high-tail it out of Oregon across the Astoria Bridge, taking the less-traveled coastal route.

At first light, they'd ditch Jo Jo's Corolla and grab a new car with Washington plates. They'd make their way across the Canadian border at an unwatched crossing Bud had used before. About four long days of driving followed by a ferry ride and they'd be in Kodiak.

Jessie would have her baby, and Bud and Jo Jo would sit on their front porch in his-and-her Adirondack chairs watching deer stroll by.

So why was he so afraid?

His right hand, the one holding his coffee mug, started shaking. He had to use his left to lower the mug to the table. It landed with a thud, spilling a few drops.

The warning signs were clear as could be, but Bud steadied himself.

He'd be a criminal once more. Out of love.

———

When they got to the house, they saw the lawyer's black BMW in the driveway next to the minivan. The light in the baby's room was still on.

So they waited.

A few minutes after 8, Bud caught a fleeting glimpse of the woman in the upstairs window. She was bending over what he figured was the baby's crib.

"It's almost time," he said to Jo Jo, who saw the same thing.

Bud grabbed his bag and put it on his lap. He was pleased there was no full moon that could make it harder to approach the house undetected.

The houses on either side of the couple's home were dark. That, too, was a bit of good fortune.

The upstairs light went out.

"Wish me luck," Bud said, and Jo Jo gave him a kiss on the cheek.

"Be careful."

He nodded and opened the car door. She watched as he walked quickly across the street and disappeared in the dark by the garage.

Bud pulled out a small pry bar to force the lock but when he tested the knob, it turned.

Doing exactly what he had rehearsed in his mind, he put on his black ski mask with holes for his eyes and mouth. He put on his leather gloves and pulled the gun from his waistband.

Turning the knob as slowly as he could, he eased the door open a crack. He could hear the man and woman talking in another room.

As stealthily as he could, Bud stepped inside the kitchen and made his way around a large granite-topped island. He peeked around a wall and saw the couple seated on a couch, sipping wine. She was asking him about his day.

They seemed like fine people, and Bud felt a twinge of regret in what he was about to do. He reminded himself that for the first time in his life he'd be stealing something without a trace of greed.

It's a righteous crime.

He paused to ready himself, then stepped into the living room, his gun trained on the couple.

They didn't notice him at first. Then the woman screamed and dropped her glass, spilling red wine on the carpet. The man looked at the gun and blood drained from his face.

"Take whatever you want. Please, just don't shoot," he said, pulling off an expensive watch and placing it on the table.

"I won't hurt you," Bud told the terrified couple. "Just stay quiet and do exactly what I say."

The hand holding the gun began trembling and he hoped they didn't notice.

"I need you to go down the stairs to the basement. I'm going to tie you up so you can't call police."

"Is this a robbery?" the man asked. He'd dropped his wallet on the table next to the watch.

"No questions. Let's go!"

He marched them down to the basement, which was unfinished except for a laundry room.

"Sit down," he commanded.

Bud noticed a vertical steel support beam next to the furnace and handcuffed them to it. Then he took duct tape and bound their feet.

"If you pull very hard on this beam, the ceiling will probably collapse," he advised. "Don't do that."

"Why are you doing this? Please just take the money," the man said.

The woman's eyes widened in fear as she remembered her sleeping baby upstairs.

"Please don't hurt our baby!"

Bud stood there, the gun and duct tape in his hands. All he had to do was gag them, grab the child and leave.

But his body was shaking and he began hyperventilating. He closed his eyes and he was back in prison. His parole had just been denied.

The guards were all laughing, telling him he'd never get out.

Never get out.

Never get out.

Never get out.

The husband watched in disbelief as Bud stood there, looking possessed.

"What's happening to him?" the wife whispered.

"I don't know. He's maybe having a stroke."

The gun slipped from Bud's quaking hand and fell to the concrete floor with a clatter. The husband desperately began reaching for it with his legs.

He managed to push the weapon toward his wife a few inches.

"Honey, see if you can get it!"

She began wiggling her feet also, kicking the gun closer. It was now just inches from the steel beam — and her husband's cuffed hand.

Just one more kick and …

"Stop!!"

Bud, snapping out of his trance, grabbed the gun off the floor and held the barrel to the man's head.

"I should blow your brains out for that," he said.

"Please! I didn't mean anything! I thought you were having a heart attack."

The woman began pleading again.

"Take what you want but please don't hurt our baby!"

Bud taped their mouths shut, then looked the woman in the eye.

"You stole the baby. I'm taking him back."

The couple exchanged confused looks and then the wife started sobbing. Her husband, unable to console her, looked at her with a profound sadness.

It was a heart-breaking scene, but Bud had a job to do.

A righteous crime.

"I need you to both stay calm. If you do that, I promise to call the police and let them know you're down here."

Bud walked up the stairs and shut the door. There was a deadbolt and he slid it into place just in case.

In the baby's room, he was relieved to find the infant still sleeping. He gently packed the boy into the couple's carrier, already lined with a soft, pale-blue blanket.

When he got to the side door, he checked to make sure nobody was around and no cars were coming. The houses next door were still dark.

Moments later, he was in the back seat of the car with the carrier.

"Let's go," he said.

"What happened? It's been a half-hour," Jo Jo said, alarmed. "Is everything okay?"

"It's all good. Go!"

She hit the gas and the car began speeding down the hill.

"Not too fast."

"What took so long?"

"I had a little … flashback."

"What? Oh my God!"

"I think tying them up in the basement triggered it, but it only lasted a few minutes."

"Oh, Bud. The couple – they didn't try to get away or anything, did they?"

"No, I think I may have scared them a little. The man thought I was having a stroke."

The baby made a contented, gurgling noise and Jo Jo managed a smile.

"You did it, Bud. You really did it."

It took just a few minutes to get to the empty lot where Jessie was waiting anxiously by her 10-year-old Subaru Outback. Bud handed her the carrier and she began to cry.

"My baby, my baby …"

She hugged Bud tightly and he gently pried her off.

"No time," he said.

Jessie transferred the still-slumbering infant to a waiting safety seat and slid behind the wheel. Jo Jo gave her a kiss and whispered something in her ear.

Then she drove off.

"What did you tell her?" Bud asked as they got back in the Corolla.

"I wished her luck."

"She'll need it. So will we."

They drove to the other side of downtown and stopped in an alley about a block behind the adoption agency office. Bud scanned the parking lot and saw it was empty, except for a black pickup truck on the far end, next to a motel.

His good fortune was continuing.

"This time, I really will be quick."

Bud put on his gloves, but didn't bother with the mask and gun, tucking the pry bar into his waistband instead.

"Keep it running."

He ran over to a rear window and quickly pried it open. Climbing inside, he was happy to not have triggered an audible alarm. For a business that dealt in large sums of ill-gotten cash, they should really invest in a security system, he thought.

He made his way to Krump's office and stepped over to her desk. He forced the drawer with the pry bar and pulled it out.

Bud froze for a few seconds, but it wasn't another stress attack. Instead of one envelope stuffed with cash, there were several.

"Holy shit!" His good luck, it seemed, had no bounds.

The thief tucked the envelopes into his hoodie and returned to the rear window.

As he was dangling out, his legs a few feet off the ground, he heard a loud crack.

The window frame suddenly exploded into pieces.

Somebody's shooting at me!

Bud dropped to the pavement and began running frantically across the lot. He looked over his shoulder and saw nobody.

He made it to the car. It was still idling, but Jo Jo wasn't there.

What the hell?

Bud looked up and down the alley but saw nothing. Maybe she was hiding from the shooter.

"Jo Jo! Jo Jo!!"

He scanned the parking lot. In the darkness he could make out the shadowy figure of a man holding what appeared to be a rifle.

Spooked, Bud jumped in the car and took off. Questions swirled in his mind.

Where did Jo Jo go? Is she okay?

There was no time to wait for answers. Someone was trying to kill him.

The Corolla roared across the bridge, thankfully deserted, and headed north. After a few frantic miles, when he was sure nobody was chasing him, Bud pulled over.

His heart was pounding, his mind reeling.

After calming himself, he decided to head back into town to look for Jo Jo. She must be hiding somewhere off that alley. He'd have his gun, and if the would-be assassin showed up again, this time he'd be prepared.

He was about to turn the car around when he noticed his girlfriend's jacket and shoulder bag were no longer on the back seat.

She must have grabbed them and ran.

Another thought popped into his head. A darker one.

He popped the trunk and walked around to look inside.

Her suitcase was also gone.

As that realization washed over him, Bud doubled over in pain.

The love of his life had betrayed him.

17

Bud's carefully constructed plan was in ruins.

His girlfriend had abandoned him, leaving him alone and on the run.

He'd soon be branded a notorious ex-con who got out of prison and immediately began plotting to abduct a baby from a respectable couple.

It would be called a heinous crime, and not just by police, the press and the baby's adoptive parents, but by virtually anyone with a pulse.

Bud knew there would be a furious manhunt, the likes of which probably hadn't been seen since March 1, 1932, when 20-month-old Charles Augustus Lindbergh Jr. was snatched from his crib on the second floor of his New Jersey home.

The Lindbergh kidnapping, Bud knew from his readings behind bars, ended very badly – with the child's slaying and the arrest of Bruno Hauptmann, a German immigrant who had demanded a ransom in a crude note left on the bedroom windowsill. After what was dubbed the "Trial of the Century," Hauptmann was convicted of capital murder, sentenced to death and electrocuted.

Would the Baker baby-napping be considered just as dastardly?

Hopefully not – not after all the facts came out. But Bud wasn't a big believer on relying on better angels in dire situations and his situation was indeed dire. At this very moment, Jo Jo could be pinning all the blame on him and tipping off authorities to his escape route.

And then there was the indisputable fact that somebody out there was trying to kill him.

Parked on a muddy shoulder off Highway 101 just south of the hamlet of Ilwaco, Washington, Bud scanned the road for any suspicious vehicles that might be carrying a man with a high-powered rifle. Seeing none, he resumed his fretting.

For a moment, he considered changing course and heading to Las Vegas, where he could hunt down the sisters and exact a little revenge. But what would that revenge be? A tongue-lashing? Taking the baby back?

Shaking his head, he blamed himself for not realizing that Jo Jo had been pretending to love him so he'd kidnap her sister's baby.

What a fool I was!

He remembered Jo Jo whispering something to her sister before they drove to the adoption office. Was she telling her to pick her up there as soon as he was inside the building?

And if so, why hadn't she waited until he returned with the money and robbed the robber? His gun had been in the car.

He pounded his chest in frustration and heard a strange crinkling sound.

He'd forgotten about the money.

After checking for his hunter one more time, he pulled the fat envelopes out of his hoodie and dumped the cash onto the passenger seat. He stared at the pile of crisp hundred-dollar bills in amazement.

Holy crap!

The outlaw counted the Benjamins and gulped. An even $50,000.

More than enough to get killed over.

As he opened the glove box to make sure his gun was still there, he saw a note inside.

It was from Jo Jo, written by hand in blue ink:

"Dear Bud, when you read this you will be upset and deservedly so. I had to go with Jessie, to protect her and the baby. I know I made promises to you, and I hate myself for leaving like this, but I hope you can at least try to understand. Please know that I love you, J."

Despite his still-boiling anger, Bud lowered his head and cried – something he hadn't done in a very long time. Maybe not since his father left.

It took minutes to collect his wits. He stuffed the note in his front jeans pocket, then loaded the cash in his bag.

Firing up the car, he resolved to stick with the plan, only without his red-haired accomplice. He'd continue north to Alaska.

The plan, however, didn't account for a man with a rifle. Who was he? An off-duty cop? A thug hired by Little Angels?

Bud had no idea. Steering the Corolla back onto the highway, he looked at his watch and winced. He needed to get moving.

Cops would be looking for a man, at least at first. If any neighbors had seen the red car parked outside the Astoria home on the hill the night of the break-in, they'd be looking for it, too.

Bud had settled on an escape plan that avoided the quickest route – Interstate 5, slicing through Olympia, Tacoma and Seattle – in favor of Highway 101, the scenic two-lane road that would take him along the rugged coastline, bordering the Quinault Indian Reservation and skirting the Olympic Mountains to the east.

If all went well, the fugitive would be in Port Angeles, on the Strait of Juan de Fuca, by morning. The next stop would be the U.S.-Canada border. And then on to the wilds of Alaska.

Where, God willing, he could get lost forever.

———

Bud could hear the ocean's thunder when he first saw the headlights.

It was still dark outside but with a flicker of illumination around the edges, the first hints of sunrise. The driver rubbed his eyes and heard his stomach growl. He decided to stop at a diner in Port Angeles, about 90 miles up the road.

But first there was the problem in his rear-view mirror.

The headlights were getting bigger.

Bud's instinct was to slow down, in case it was a cop. But as the dark shape of the vehicle behind him came into focus, he realized a large pickup truck was barreling down on him.

At 5 a.m., it was unlikely to be a drunken driver, but Bud felt his neck and shoulders tensing.

Oh, c'mon, relax. Just someone in a hurry.

He began slowing down to let the truck pass when he remembered seeing a big black pickup in the parking lot near the adoption agency – from roughly where that man shot at him.

The headlights were even bigger now.

Panicked, Bud reversed course and hit the gas. The Toyota shook and shimmied as its speed reached 80 mph.

The old highway was slick with fresh rain and he struggled to keep the light sedan on the road. He was grateful to be hugging the forest side of the highway – if he had been traveling south, there would be sheer cliffs dropping to the ocean below immediately to his right.

As he fishtailed around a curve, he looked in the mirror. The truck was still gaining on him.

It was an older model Ford F-250 and it had made up so much ground that now Bud could see the huge front grill with its horizontal chrome bars. He looked for the driver but couldn't make him out in the glare of those big rectangular headlights.

He's going to ram me!

In the mirror, Bud, now terrified, saw nothing but chrome as the Ford, propelled by its 300-horsepower V8, rammed the back of the much smaller Toyota. The sedan lurched forward, but Bud managed to hold it steady.

He tried flooring it, but the car protested and the Ford rammed it a second time, only much harder.

Bud heard the sound of crumpling metal, followed by a sickening feeling as the compact car began spinning out of control. The Toyota did a 180-degree turn, now facing the truck.

In the middle of the two-lane road, Bud could only shut his eyes and hold on for dear life as the pickup clipped the front end of the sedan.

The car spun again, reversing itself, but this time it slid across the road and over the side.

Bud screamed as the Toyota plunged off the cliff and into a cluster of pines growing out of the rocks. Miraculously, the vehicle was slowed by the trees, sheering off branches as it fell.

Then about halfway down it stopped – or rather paused. Bud could hear the trees bowing and creaking from the weight and knew he'd only have a few seconds to escape.

Get out! Get out!!

Bud grabbed his bag and opened the driver's door. There was still an 80-foot drop to the ocean and a beach dotted with massive boulders.

"Fuck!"

There was no time to get his gun out of the glove box. He'd be left to protect himself with only a pocketknife and his fists.

He managed to climb out onto the tree, hugging it for dear life. Moments later, several large branches snapped and the Toyota plummeted. It struck one of the largest boulders like a bomb, blasting apart and bursting into flames.

Bud was still clinging to the swaying tree like a scared monkey. He couldn't tell which was shaking more.

For several minutes, he stayed there, high in a tree, paralyzed by fear. He closed his eyes and willed himself to not have another anxiety attack.

Then he heard a throaty rumble and looked below. The powerful pickup had made it down to the silty brown beach.

He couldn't see much – it wasn't quite dawn yet – but he made out the silhouette of a man in a cowboy hat walking over to the Corolla's smoking ruins.

He's checking to see if I'm dead. Jesus Christ.

Despite his panic, Bud convinced himself to get back up to the road somehow. If he stayed in the tree, he'd be easy pickings for an assassin with a rifle once the sun was up.

The nearest tree rubbed against the cliff and still had its upper branches intact. He strapped on the backpack and leaped for it.

The outlaw reached the tree easily. It must have been his adrenalin kicking in.

The black truck was driving away. He'd have to move fast before the hunter returned to the coastal highway to start tracking him again.

Bud climbed up the tree branch by branch until he could jump to solid ground. The sun had risen and he was exposed. He sprinted across the road and into a stand of pines to hide.

He thought about his predicament and shook his head.

Not only was he hungry and tired, but he was likely being hunted by cops of all stripes plus a maniacal cowboy.

In a perverse way, he envied Jo Jo. She was probably halfway to Vegas by now, playing with the baby and listening to pop music CDs.

He felt a strange brew of sadness and anger rising within him and that was good. He needed more than adrenalin to keep him going.

Weaving through the misty forest, he made his way north.

18

$\mathbf{R}$oadblock.

"Oh my God," Jessie breathed as cars ahead of her began to brake.

She and Jo Jo saw a police car with flashing lights blocking the road, less than a quarter-mile ahead. An officer was questioning drivers.

"Check the map, JJ," the worried driver said. "Is this the Nevada border?"

Jo Jo unfolded the map and shook her head.

"No, we're about 20 miles away, in the middle of nowhere. Nearest town is Burns Junction."

"Then why a roadblock here?"

They had left the main highway hours ago to avoid detection, as Bud had recommended. This road, while technically a state route, was curvy and narrow, with one lane in each direction.

Jessie glanced at the back seat and saw her newly recovered baby, nestled in his powder-blue blanket, cooing in the safety seat.

"What do we do with him?" The mother hadn't chosen a name yet, so she only used pronouns.

"We put him in the trunk – he'll be okay for a few minutes."

"Yeah, but he's wide awake. If he starts crying …"

"Pull over," the older sister said firmly. "Let's figure this out."

Jo Jo wished Bud was with them. He'd have a plan for this situation.

"Maybe we should turn back and try another road," she said.

Jessie slapped her forehead, hoping to force out some good ideas. "How many hours has it been since we left Astoria?" she asked.

Jo Jo looked at her watch.

"Nine hours, give or take."

"Nine hours? I thought Bud said we'd have a head start of 24 hours – at least."

"He did, but maybe something happened. Maybe the couple escaped and called police."

"Or maybe Bud called police because of what you did," Jessie said.

"He wouldn't do that."

"He's a criminal, and a smart one. Don't think for a minute that your little note solved anything. He's pissed and he turned us in."

"Stop it! Bud may be angry, but he'd never do that."

The sisters sat in the Subaru on the side of the road, watching cars pull up to the roadblock. Some drove on while others turned around.

"I think we just have to risk it," Jo Jo said finally.

"And if the baby cries? And if they ask for our IDs? What do we do then?"

"Damn it, Jessie, we have no choice. I think Bud was right. We have 24 hours. Let's just do it."

Jessie sighed.

"You're right. I don't want to give up or do something stupid, not when we're so close. I mean, we'll be in Nevada in a half-hour!"

And then, just as they agreed to continue on to the roadblock, a higher spirit intervened. They looked back at the baby and he was asleep.

He briefly stirred when they transferred him to the carrier, but then his eyes fluttered shut again. They waited until there was no car coming up behind them then gently placed the carrier in the trunk along with the safety seat.

They closed the trunk as quietly as they could and waited, listening, for a few seconds. There were no cries.

The sisters hugged each other and returned to their seats.

"We're visiting friends in Reno," Jo Jo said.

"Got it," Jessie said. Her fingers were trembling on the steering wheel, turquoise nails making a tapping sound.

She took a deep breath and rolled down her window. The state trooper leaned in and looked around.

"Afternoon, ladies. Where are you headed?"

"Visiting friends in Reno," Jessie said, doing her best to smile.

"What puts you on this road?" the trooper asked. "It's a lot faster to take the interstate."

"That's what I told her!" Jo Jo said, pretending to be annoyed.

The trooper's stony facade didn't change.

"Well, we just had a small plane make an emergency landing on the road up ahead," he said. "Until we can get it towed, we're asking people to either turn around or pull up to a waiting area about 50 yards ahead."

The sisters looked at each other, trying not to act too relieved.

"Oh, we'll wait. Thank you, officer," Jessie said.

"Good day, ladies. Travel safe."

They drove ahead and, just like the trooper said, there was a grassy field off the road where a dozen or so vehicles – most of them farmers' pickups – were waiting. The sisters could see emergency crews around the plane, a Beechcraft Skipper with smoke rising from its engine.

Jessie parked and, after making sure no one was watching, raced around the car to grab her son. His bright blue eyes were wide open.

"Hey, sis, sorry about what I said about Bud and the note and stuff," she said as she set up the safety seat.

"Apology accepted."

Within minutes, the plane had been pushed far enough to the side that one lane of traffic could reopen. A short time later, the sisters drove past the "Welcome to Nevada" sign.

"Hallelujah!" Jessie yelled.

"Vegas here we come!" Jo Jo exclaimed.

They laughed so hard tears rolled down their cheeks.

The baby laughed, too.

———

Bud hiked along the timbered ridge above the highway. He didn't see the black truck again, but he knew it was out there somewhere.

He couldn't risk hitching a ride. He'd just have to keep walking and stay out of sight.

The sun was directly overhead when he broke through some trees and saw rooftops in the distance. The fugitive walked past meadows dotted with wildflowers and approached the small town warily.

It was Forks, just outside the Olympic National Forest. His stomach growled in protest as he kept moving. He'd only had a handful of half-ripe berries in the past 24 hours and had to eat something.

The highway ran through town and when Bud got there, he saw a diner on a street corner that looked open. After searching up and down for black pickups, he walked over to Nellie's Nest and stepped inside.

He sat down in a booth facing the door and ordered a double bacon cheeseburger and fries. When the food hit the table a few minutes later, he devoured it quickly.

When the waitress stopped by with her pot of coffee, Bud's plate was so clean she had to smile.

"Anything else?" she asked.

Bud nodded. He asked for a slice of marionberry pie with a scoop of vanilla ice cream and black coffee.

As the tension slowly drained from him, he looked out the windows and saw a purple-and-black Jeep Laredo parked outside with a "For Sale" sign on it.

It had the old school grill with close-set round headlights and a sturdy, flat-chrome bumper. Best of all, it was built for snow and rugged terrain with knobby tires and high fenders.

After paying for his meal, he found a spot behind the diner where he could wait for the owner of the Jeep to return without being seen.

Thirty minutes later, a middle-aged man wearing denim overalls and a faded ballcap appeared. Bud approached casually, reminding himself to be cool.

"Hey, man, what year is your CJ-7?"

The man brightened.

"2006. Interested?"

"Depends. How much?"

"I'm asking $4,000."

"Mind if I take a look?"

Bud walked around the freshly waxed and scrubbed off-road vehicle and nodded in appreciation. The interior looked flawless.

"Nice body. Miles?"

"Less than 70,000," the man said, looking a bit sad. "I hate to give her up, but my wife wants something a little fancier."

"I like it rough. Tell you what, I'll give you $5,000 in cash – if I can take her right now."

The man looked like he had just won the jackpot.

"Sold!"

Minutes later, the deal done, Bud climbed in his new ride, waved goodbye to the happy man counting his cash and drove up the street.

He saw a clothing store and pulled into one of the diagonal spaces in front. He bought a change of clothes, gloves and a fleece-lined denim jacket that would help him keep warm on frosty evenings.

Then Bud climbed in the Jeep. He was about to pull out when his heart skipped. A large black pickup truck was cruising down the road.

He lowered himself in his seat as the F-250 passed, heading south toward where he had entered the town. He dared a peek and saw a weathered American flag decal on the tailgate and Idaho plates streaked with mud.

He couldn't see the driver's face but saw the outline of a cowboy hat.

Who the hell is this guy?

There was no question in Bud's mind that the man was hunting him. Twice, he had tried to kill him, and the fugitive didn't want to risk a third encounter.

Bud drove the opposite direction headed north, hoping to put some distance between himself and his would-be killer. This was no amateur, he knew. He was too calm, too methodical, too skilled with a rifle and scope.

Fueled by the coffee, he forced himself to think. He reviewed the facts. The man shot at him after he robbed Little Angels, so he had either followed Bud there or was lying in wait.

But why would an adoption agency, even a corrupt one, need a hired gun? Were they a bigger criminal enterprise than he thought? Was it organized crime? Did the man with the rifle work for the mob?

There was another possibility. A disturbing one.

Maybe Jo Jo wanted him killed. Maybe she hired the assassin and told him Bud's plans – had him waiting in the parking lot when he came out of the window.

But then why did she leave the note? And the car?

Why didn't she just have him killed and then take the money from the robbery before leaving with her sister?

Bud shook his head. It didn't make sense.

Then again, how would the killer know to find him up north on the Washington coast?

His mind kept going back to the American flag decal that was chipped and faded. The Idaho plates. The cowboy hat.

It just didn't seem like the kind of things a man who relied on stealth would do. They seemed like, well, clues. Identifiers. Maybe the gunman wasn't all that professional, after all.

Maybe he'll give up and leave me alone.

He turned on the stereo and was perturbed to find nothing but static on the FM dial. He'd be in Port Angeles shortly. Should he risk getting a room for the night or press on to the border?

There were so many questions.

His head ached and his eyelids were heavy. He'd been on the run for 24 hours but it felt like a week. He doubted whether he'd survive another day of being hunted.

Bud swerved to a stop at a roadside motel. He checked in and pulled the Jeep around back so it couldn't be seen from the highway. There was a liquor store next door, so he went in and bought a bottle of rum and a couple of cans of Coke.

As he was about to turn the key in the door of his first-floor room, he suddenly found himself caught in a spotlight.

Thinking it could be cops training their guns on him, he slowly turned and saw something almost as terrifying – the headlights of a large black pickup moving toward him.

Bud reached for his gun only to realize he didn't have one.

The truck stopped and the driver's door swung open.

A round man with a long white beard stepped out with a grunt. From the passenger seat a grandmotherly woman emerged. She gave Bud a friendly smile.

"Nice night, isn't it?" she said.

The fugitive watched the couple walk away and leaned heavily against the door. How much of this could he take?

In his room, he made himself a stiff drink, which he downed in two gulps. He took a deep breath, then grabbed the phone and made the call that could lead directly to his arrest.

When a man answered, Bud said as calmly as he could, "This is important. Please write this down."

"Go ahead."

"Send a unit to 2525 Worthington Avenue. A big house on the hill. There's a couple handcuffed in the basement."

"Did you say 'handcuffed'?"

"That's right. Send someone now."

Bud hung up.

He had promised the lawyer and his wife he'd call the cops, but he wasn't entirely sure if he'd actually do it when the time came. He didn't get the head start he'd hoped for, thanks to a couple of assassination attempts and hours of unscripted hiking.

The old Bud – the one who robbed until he was caught – wouldn't have done it. The new Bud – the one having stress attacks, nightmares and flashbacks – was a different man.

Lock someone up in a hopeless place with hardened criminals for 25 years and suddenly set him free, and one of two things will happen, as Bud saw it. That person would either commit more crimes, possibly even worse ones, or rise above his past, becoming a better human being.

Some would call the latter "going straight" or being rehabilitated. Bud wasn't sure where he fit in the scheme of things.

Yes, he'd just tied up and robbed people, just like he used to, but this time he didn't do it for personal gain. He did it out of love and compassion and a sense of moral justice – as foolish as that now seemed.

So even though he'd just called the Astoria Police Department, triggering a manhunt, he thought it was the right thing to do.

Wasn't it?

19

Across the strait's cerulean waters, Bud could see the vague outlines of Canadian land, his pathway to Alaska.

But he drove past the dock that could have taken him via car ferry to Vancouver Island, British Columbia, saving valuable time. He didn't have a passport and, more importantly, was a fugitive, likely described in urgent police bulletins as "armed and extremely dangerous."

The bulletins would also say he had a hostage: A blue-eyed baby boy.

To avoid detection, or at least lessen the risk, he'd have to make his way northeast to the border, eschewing major highways and ferries patrolled by cops.

He figured he'd reach his remote border path by nightfall, using the Jeep to traverse a hill dotted with rocks and pines.

The man hunting him would most likely be waiting for him outside Blaine, Washington, just south of the main U.S.-Canada crossing. So, Bud planned to cross about 20 miles to the east.

He glanced at his watch and wondered if Jo Jo and Jessie had made it safely to Vegas with the baby. Despite everything, he hoped they had. He had risked so much to give them the chance to start over.

It was April and the fields were bursting with golden daffodils and red-and-white tulips. Some were commercial crops, soon to be harvested and shipped, but a few seemed to exist purely for the pleasure of anyone who happened to pass by.

The new Bud noticed and smiled.

Just then, a patrol car headed his way on the narrow country road. Bud tensed, his knuckles on the steering wheel turning white.

But the deputy rolled past, and Bud bravely gave the man a nod.

Feeling lucky, he wove his way through back roads until he reached the border at sundown. Leaving the last stretch of paved road, he drove the Laredo up an embankment to a grassy knoll. The headlights showed a gap in some towering pines he could squeeze through.

With only inches to spare on each side, he slowly guided the vehicle through the gap and into a grassy field. In the distance, he could see the top of an old red barn.

He was in Canada.

Halfway to freedom.

Bud drove down the hill and found a narrow road. He passed a few farms and ranches before the asphalt widened and bore stripes.

A short time later, he found himself entering a tiny hamlet. The commercial area was no more than two blocks long, consisting mostly of a general store, post office, diner and gas station that doubled as an auto body repair shop.

Bud pulled up to a pump and began filling the Jeep.

A young man with long stringy hair and a patchy beard came running out from the shop.

"Need any help?"

"I'm good," Bud said, but then reconsidered. "Hey, is there a decent place to eat in town?"

"Shirley's is good," he said, pointing down the street.

"Thanks, I'll check it out. Any big black pickups pass through in the last couple of hours?"

"I've got one on the lift right now."

Bud looked over and was relieved to see a Canadian license plate.

"That's not the one I'm worried about," he told the attendant, who shrugged at the strange remark and returned to his tire-rotation duties.

The hunted man walked over to the restaurant and ordered a turkey club and coffee.

When he was done, he stepped outside onto the Old West-style boardwalk fronting the businesses. He did a couple of stretches to limber up for the next leg of his journey. And then he jumped.

"Holy shit!"

Across the street, parked in front of the general store, was a black F-250.

No fucking way! Not in Canada!

Bud dashed back into the café and peeked out the window.

"Are you okay, honey?" a voice called out.

He turned to see the gray-haired waitress standing behind him, a stack of dirty plates in one hand.

"Just trying to avoid someone. Ex-wife."

"They're the worst," she said with a grimace, then disappeared through a swinging door into the kitchen.

Bud looked back at the truck and gulped. Idaho plates. American flag decal.

He slumped against the door and tried to think. How could this man have tracked him here, in the middle of nowhere? He didn't even know the name of this flyspeck town, and his special crossing spot was a closely guarded secret.

Bud heard a rumbling sound and turned back to the window. The truck was gone.

Hoping to get some answers, he walked across the street to the general store. He hailed the man behind the counter whose face was buried in the local newspaper.

"Excuse me, but my friend – the one in the cowboy hat – was just here."

"That's right," the elderly shopkeeper said. He was bald with small round glasses perched on the edge of his nose resembling a misplaced accountant.

"He's a little on the forgetful side. Sometimes, I have to check to make sure he got what I told him to get."

"That so?"

"Yeah. It's a bitch, checking on him all the time."

The man looked pained. "Well, they say old age isn't for the faint of heart. But this fellow – *your friend* – he seemed pretty sharp."

"He has his moments. What did he buy?"

"Cartridges for a Springfield 'ought-six. Said he was doing some big game hunting."

"That's the plan." *But it's not moose he's gunning for.* "Thanks, sorry to bother."

"Good luck, son. I'll always have a soft spot in my heart for lawmen."

"Yeah, I … what did you say?"

"Good luck."

"No, after that."

"Oh. He said he used to be a sheriff in the States, but you knew that, right?"

"Right."

"We get hunters through here fairly regular. Good elk and moose country. You a hunter, too?"

"No, I'm more like the prey," Bud deadpanned as he walked out.

"Americans," the man groused, picking up his paper.

Bud noticed a phone booth around the corner. He stepped inside and pulled the folded door shut. He plunked in some coins and made a call.

A familiar voice answered.

"Roger Sweet, Statesman newsroom."

"Hey man, this is Bud."

"Bud! The free man! How's it going?"

"Well, not so well at the moment. Look, I'm at a pay phone and I only have a minute. This may sound nuts, but somebody is trying to kill me. A former sheriff, I think. Ran my car off the road, shot at me with a sniper rifle."

"*What?*"

"Any of that ring a bell?"

"No, none of it."

"Well, look, nobody digs into shit better than you. Can you ask around? This guy drives a big Ford pickup with Idaho plates. Wears a cowboy hat."

"You've seen him?"

"Not his face, but he's getting closer all the time."

"C'mon Bud, this sounds far-fetched. Have you been drinking?"

"Man, I swear to God: This dude is hunting me."

"Where are you?"

"Middle of nowhere. Just crossed the Canada border, heading to Alaska, and he was just here buying ammo for Chrissakes. My time is almost up. Please see what you can find out. You can leave a message for me at Frontier Ridge General Store in Kodiak."

"Frontier Ridge … got it," Sweet said, writing it down. "Stay safe Bud, I'll make a few calls. And, remember, you owe me a post-release interview."

"Pray for me, dude. It's not easy being free."

20

When Bud called, Sweet was writing another Page One story.

He was in the middle of covering a murder trial in which a man who flipped burgers for a living snapped after being fired and returned to the restaurant to gun down several co-workers, including the person who canned him.

The case had ended in guilty verdicts for multiple counts of aggravated murder and now was in the penalty phase, with defense lawyers, after doing little to contest the prosecution's case, vigorously trying to spare their client's life by portraying him as an abused psychopath.

This was all big news for Boiseans, so Sweet had little time to make calls on Bud's behalf.

Fortunately for the fugitive, the jury deliberated for less than three hours before sending the defendant to Death Row at Bud's former residence.

After filing the story, Sweet was true to his word. He called his source at the governor's office and the Ada County sheriff, with whom he had formed a trusting relationship after Sweet's series on unexplained jail deaths led to reforms.

Neither had any idea what Bud Baker was talking about, but they seemed to enjoy the fact that he was being harassed.

The reporter then tried the Corrections spokesman, who, while a noxious, self-serving weasel, was afraid of getting on Sweet's bad side. The Baker-based court order that put the Idaho state prison system under federal watch was still partially in effect.

"Check with Alex Cooper," the flack said, almost in a whisper. "He said something about meeting with an old sheriff about Baker. That's all I know. May be nothing at all."

Sweet thanked him and hung up.

Cooper was the head of the parole board that had denied Bud's release a few months ago. It would have been surprising if the board, stacked with conservatives, had set the convict free. Sweet himself assumed it was a foregone conclusion and chose not to drive out to the desert to cover it. He wound up writing a brief that ran inside the local news section.

Cooper's real job was working for the Republican Party as a fundraiser for local and state races. He was young and ambitious, and no doubt would make his first bid for political office soon.

Sweet made the call with little hope of getting anything useful.

When Cooper answered, the reporter introduced himself and said he was thinking about doing a follow-up story on Baker.

"I figured he'd be arrested by now," Cooper scoffed. "He should never have been released."

"I can understand why you feel that way. The governor undermined your decision."

"It's more than that. I really think he poses a risk to the public. You can quote me."

"I suppose time will tell, right?"

"That's right."

"Alex, I heard that after he was released you had a face-to-face about it with a former sheriff. Is that true?"

"Oh, you mean Withers?"

"I don't know that name."

"Sure you do: Frank Withers of Owyhee County. He caught that famous outlaw, about 30 years ago. Hunted him in the hills, found him hiding in a cave. Quite a shootout, but Withers got his man. Made the cover of Newsweek, I think."

"Yeah, now I remember. Outlaw named Scraggs, killed a game warden and a rancher."

"Big story."

"Before my time at the paper, unfortunately. Hey, what did you and Withers talk about?"

"Not much, he really just wanted to vent about Baker's release. Never saw a man so furious."

"Why's that?"

"Oh, come on, Roger, you're pulling my leg."

"No, seriously, I have no idea."

"Withers is the father of the deputy who died when they arrested Baker."

"That deputy had the last name Caruso, not Withers," Sweet said. "I read the clips."

"That's right. The boy was Withers' stepson, but the only child he had. Followed in his father's footsteps and went into law enforcement. And when he died, the family's misery only grew. Wither's wife took her life a couple of weeks later. It's all in the 'victim's statement' letters he wrote to the commission."

"So, Withers has blamed Baker for his son's death and his wife's suicide all these years?"

"Yep."

"Even though the investigation proved the deputy died from friendly fire and the murder charge was dismissed?"

"That doesn't matter. Withers is convinced his son would be alive today if it wasn't for Baker, and he's probably right."

"That was 25 years ago. A long time to hold a grudge."

"True. He was re-elected sheriff a couple more times, but he stepped down eight years ago or so. Said he just couldn't do it anymore. People say he visits his wife's grave every day, talks to her out loud like she's still alive.

"Anyway, when they let Baker out in the middle of the night, the old sheriff went nuts. Got thrown out of the Capitol after threatening the governor. I talked to him a couple of days later, and he was still angry as hell."

Sweet suddenly realized it was Withers who had called him in a rage about his story on Bud's release.

"Tell me about your chat."

"Roger, that's confidential. Talk to Withers if you have to know."

"C'mon Alex, off the record. I won't write about it, I'm just curious."

"Off the record?"

"I promise."

"Okay, well, one thing kinda stands out. Withers was just venting, like I said, and then he said something a little strange. He asked me if Baker had a release plan. He wanted to see it. I asked him why, and he had this wild look in his eye and said, 'I have something to tell him.' And then I remembered Baker had a sponsor in Kodiak, Alaska, and I told Withers that, and he got up and said, 'Much obliged.' Then he left. That was it."

"You said Kodiak?"

"Yeah, why?"

"I think the sheriff is going after Baker and not just to talk to him."

"What do you mean?"

"Did Withers wear a cowboy hat when you talked to him?"

"He always does. Light brown with a blue leather band. Why?"

"Baker called me yesterday. He said a man with a cowboy hat and a black pickup truck with Idaho plates has been hunting him all the way from Oregon."

"You don't believe that crap, do you? *Hunted?* Come on. He's playing you."

"I didn't believe it – until just now when you told me how obsessed Withers is."

"You think he's going to kill Baker?"

"I think he's going to try."

"Jesus, what have I done?"

Sweet suddenly felt sorry for the parole board chair.

"Hey, maybe you're right. Maybe I am being played."

Then he thanked Cooper and hung up.

Sweet walked over to the newsroom library – the old part that hadn't yet been converted into digital files, with rows and rows of shelves lined with envelopes stuffed with folded clippings. Some were organized by names, others by places or events. Journalists called it the "morgue," which seemed more than appropriate given how many of the files were on people who were no longer alive.

The librarian saw Sweet scouring the racks and came over to assist, mostly to prevent the reporter from messing things up.

"Nancy, I need everything we have on Frank Withers, former Owyhee County sheriff."

In less than a minute, she handed several thick envelopes to the reporter. She gave Sweet a stern look.

"Keep them neat."

"Don't I always?"

Sweet returned to his desk and began reading about Withers. The cattle rancher-turned-sheriff was last written about when he stepped down, refusing to grant an interview. The last time he was mentioned in the paper before that was when he won his last term, again refusing to comment publicly.

The journalist unfolded the yellowed clipping about the funeral of Johnny Caruso and saw, in the photo snapped that day, misery etched in the sheriff's face. At the graveside, his wife was limp with grief.

Her mouth was open and Sweet could practically hear her wailing.

There was a rare quote in the story from Withers that made Sweet sit back in his chair.

"I hope Baker roasts in hell," the sheriff spat. "He deserves a bullet in the head."

The reporter knew for sure then that a deranged, vengeful ex-sheriff was tracking Bud – all the way to the Alaskan wilderness if need be.

If only Bud had just stayed behind bars where it was safer.

21

It was only a matter of time now. And patience, he had been taught, benefits the hunter.

The former sheriff opened the case and pulled out his prized Springfield. Its walnut stock gleamed in the unfiltered Canadian sun. The long black barrel was cold and smooth.

Withers pushed up his wool Stetson and removed his wire-rimmed Ray-Bans. He looked through the scope, the rifle slung across the hood of the Ford.

He made some adjustments, sharpening the focus on a stretch of road 500 yards away.

Baker would be coming, he knew. The convict was eager – *desperate* – to get to Kodiak, and this twisting narrow highway was the fastest way to get there.

There was a snow marker planted in the shoulder with a reflector on it, and the sheriff put it in the cross-hairs.

Keeping the target centered in the sight, he slowly pushed the bolt up and back. He placed a .30-06 round in the chamber and locked it in place.

His right index finger rested on the trigger. He steadied his breathing. Then he squeezed.

There was a loud crack like a miniature sonic boom. And then nothing.

The marker was gone, as if it had never existed.

Withers imagined shooting Baker in the head as he drove toward him. He'd like nothing better than to see the criminal's skull explode.

"Then it will be over," he said, looking skyward. "Finally over."

Twice, his prey had escaped him. Luck had been on Baker's side then, but that would not be the case now. Withers had chosen the perfect location for an ambush, a grassy hilltop overlooking the only long straightaway on the frontier highway.

A clean shot.

As if to test his theory, a semi popped into view about a mile out. He waited, patiently, for the truck to draw closer. As it approached the kill spot, he zeroed in on the driver. He could hear the rig now.

The driver was in his cross-hairs. His finger was on the trigger.

"Bang," the old man said.

He was thinking rationally, logically, precisely — as he had all along. The weak-kneed governor had called him "crazy." The pathetic man from the parole board looked at him funny. But he wasn't crazy. He had a plan, and he would prevail. He would get justice.

Withers was at the parole hearing when Baker was denied release. For the state of Idaho to then set him free, well, it was a travesty. It could not stand. And if nobody else could rectify the situation, he damn sure would.

It didn't take long for the expert tracker to follow the convict's trail through Oregon. He knew state officials had put him on a bus bound for the coast. Astoria was the last stop. So, he drove to the riverfront city and, before long, found his prey.

The sonofabitch wasn't even hiding.

He watched in cold fury as Baker sat on a pier, enjoying life. His anger grew when he saw his target strolling along the waterfront, holding hands with a woman.

When he encountered Baker on a downtown sidewalk later that day, he couldn't resist clipping the smaller man with his shoulder, making him spill his fancy coffee drink. But the convict merely apologized for getting in the way and smiled.

The lawman, still imposing at 6-foot-2 and 225 pounds, could have killed him any number of times, but he was too skilled a hunter to rush. He would savor the hunt instead. He'd *enjoy* it.

Withers had been living in a downtown motel, a few blocks from Baker's apartment building. There, he began plotting the execution he had been so terribly denied. The only question was where. Here or in Alaska, where there would likely be no witnesses?

It was a Friday night and he was looking outside his window over the parking lot when he saw a man breaking into the building next door. As the man pulled himself into a rear window, Withers had a gut feeling it might be the robber he was hunting.

He didn't want to kill Baker this way, from behind, but there was something infuriating about watching him about to rob an office – a Christian adoption agency, of all places. He was too much of a lawman to let it stand.

The sheriff stepped outside and calmly pulled the rifle out of his truck. He loaded a bullet and waited. The lot was deserted, which only encouraged him more.

In his scope he saw two legs pop out, then an ass. Withers had the man in his cross-hairs but he had to be sure it was Baker.

Moments later, the burglar was nearly out of the window. He turned his head slightly, gauging the distance to the ground, and Withers caught a glimpse. It was Baker all right.

He pulled the trigger and the window frame shattered.

Baker had moved at precisely the wrong instant.

Withers watched as his prey sprinted away to a waiting car. He didn't fire another shot. He was a hunter and hunters are patient. He put the rifle back in its case and slid it behind the driver's seat. He glanced around and was pleased to see that despite the noise, nobody was looking.

The sheriff smiled in a steely way. He knew where Baker was going and he wasn't in a rush. Time, in fact, was his ally.

Running him off the highway was a mistake. He caught up to the felon on a coastal road and couldn't resist pushing the car off the cliff with his beastly truck.

Withers would later scold himself for not thinking more clearly, for letting bloodlust cloud his judgment.

When he realized later that Baker had somehow escaped the crash, he was full of rage. It took him hours to find the calm he needed to resume his quest.

A hunter's calm.

So now he waited. He had seen the Jeep leave the road just south of the border. He watched as it weaved through the trees. He knew that was Baker, avoiding the Canadian border guards.

He was right on his trail and now he was ready. He'd end the hunt here, before Baker could get lost in the Alaskan outback.

One shot and it would be over. One shot and his family would be avenged.

The sheriff's face was lined with deep creases, cross-hatched by age and the elements. He was 75, with thick gray hair chopped short. His blue eyes were rimmed with red, a disturbing countenance that hinted at a tormented soul. He had descended into a darkness illuminated only by the sparks of his anger.

But now, at long last, it would all be over.

With one squeeze of a trigger, his demon would be vanquished.

———

Bud had been driving for hours and not once did he see an evil black pickup.

But still he couldn't relax. Somehow, the man chasing him knew his every move. He seemed to know where he was going and when he'd get there.

And then there was that high-powered rifle. He could be sniped from a long distance, which meant that at any time he could be picked off.

Even right now.

If he could, he'd dump the money, Bud thought. Maybe then the hunter would let him be. Maybe then he could go to his cabin and be free. But another part of him knew it was too late. He'd be gunned down either way.

Soon, he'd be within sight of the southern leg of Alaska. Just the thought of that let him breathe a little easier. But getting to his part of the Last Frontier was no easy task. It would take several long days of driving to make it to Anchorage, and then to Kodiak.

A lot of time to live in fear of a sniper's bullet.

He stepped on the gas and shrugged. What else could he do? He didn't believe in God, or fate, or even karma, but taking that baby had put celestial forces in motion. He wondered what fate had in store for him.

As the miles rolled by, Bud thought about that – and a scarlet-haired woman with freckles on her nose. The woman who seemed to float on air. The woman who betrayed him but still professed her love.

The fugitive ruffled his curly hair with a free hand and whistled weakly as the Jeep sped north on Highway 37.

We all got to die sometime.

Take your best shot.

Up the road a piece, where the asphalt straightened, a hunter was waiting.

22

A team of FBI agents set up camp in downtown Astoria, taking over several rooms at the Hotel Elliott.

Leading the effort was Spencer P. Williams, a smartly dressed Black man with a thin mustache.

Nearing the end of an acclaimed career, he had accepted this assignment because, well, it was highly unusual and that made it interesting.

The Astoria case was officially an abduction involving a plump baby boy in which the perpetrators were believed to have fled across state lines.

But Williams had a knack for uncovering complex criminal conspiracies whose twists and turns weren't so easy to see. He had a nose for it, some would say.

And this baby-napping didn't add up. Starting with the lack of a ransom demand.

There was a manhunt underway but Williams knew it would fail and, a couple of days after the kidnapping, it had. Authorities in neighboring states had come up empty, which wasn't surprising given that they currently had zero suspects other than a masked man with an apparent anxiety problem.

But Williams had his gut feeling. So, while the case would normally be assigned to the Portland field office, he lobbied to journey to the scene of the crime from Chicago, bringing his partner along.

The kidnapper, as described by the baby's wealthy adoptive parents, was a white male of average height and build who wore a mask and gloves. None of the neighbors saw the suspect or his vehicle. He left no fingerprints behind.

But the armed intruder did leave a few clues. He told the adoptive parents he was "taking the baby back." He inferred he was righting a wrong.

And in the middle of tying them up in the basement, the culprit had some kind of stress attack – severe enough to drop his gun.

That's the part of the story that most intrigued Williams. Who was this strange kidnapper with a conscience?

The key, he figured, would be finding out more about the birth mother.

As he stood in front of the Little Angels building, he finished a cigarette and stomped the butt into the pavement. He had promised his wife he'd quit, but that would have to wait a little bit longer.

"None of this fits," he said to his partner, Ron Bellows. "We need some answers."

"You got that right," Bellows said.

They walked inside and showed their badges to the astonished woman at the reception desk. Seconds later, Krump emerged from her tastefully decorated office.

"How may I help you gentlemen?" she asked with a pleasant smile.

"I'm Special Agent Williams, this is Bellows. We just have a few questions."

"Is this about the abduction?"

"It is, ma'am. May we talk privately?"

"It's all just so horrible," Krump said, leading them to her office and offering the usual coffee, tea or bottled water. They politely declined.

"What can you tell us about the birth mother?" Williams asked.

"A tragic case. During her long struggle with addiction, she became pregnant. And then, when it came time to have the baby, she decided it would be best to put the child up for adoption. So, we handled that for her."

"What's her name?"

"Jessie Summers. I have her file here, if you'd like to see." She pulled a folder from a cabinet next to her desk and flipped it open.

"Here's the form she signed, authorizing the adoption," Krump said, handing the paper to Williams.

He looked it over and passed it to Bellows.

"Any idea what happened to her? Do you know her present whereabouts?"

Krump looked genuinely disappointed. "I'm so sorry. We lost contact with her after the adoption. The old address is in the file."

"I see. Mind if we borrow that?"

"Well, it is confidential, but since you gentlemen are with the FBI, I suppose we can make an exception."

Tucking the file under his arm, Williams stood to leave.

"We'll be in touch," he said.

Krump flashed a brilliant smile. "Anything I can do for you, don't hesitate to ask."

The agents' next stop was at the big house under the bridge. The landlord, a middle-aged Russian immigrant, told them Jessie had left suddenly, leaving everything behind but her clothes.

"It's a terrible thing," he said. "Losing the baby was a terrible, terrible thing. Night after night I'd hear the most awful sounds coming from her place. Sobbing and moaning. Some of the tenants complained, but I didn't have to the heart to say anything.

"I let her be – except for that one time. She tried to hang herself the day after she left the hospital. Tied a rope to that," he said, pointing at a large cedar tree. "Thank God I saw her. I cut her down and called an ambulance. She lived, but the crying didn't stop."

"Do you know where she went?"

"No. She said she was going to New York to start over, but I don't know if that was just talk."

"Any close friends here in town?" Bellows asked.

"Nah, she kept mostly to herself. But she does have an older sister. Goes by Jo Jo. Talked to her once or twice. Very nice."

Williams asked the landlord if he still had a copy of Jessie's rental contract. After a few minutes, he returned with the document.

"Thanks for your time," the FBI man said.

When the agents returned to their car, Williams compared the signature on the contract to the adoption paperwork. He showed them to his partner.

"What do you think?" he asked Bellows.

"I think we have a forgery."

"We sure do."

Besides growing concerns about Little Angels, they returned to the hotel after developing information on two persons of interest: sisters named Jessie and Jo Jo. It was highly likely that they had the baby.

But what about the man who did the job itself? Was he a hired gun, a relative or something else?

Williams and Bellows mulled that over on the hotel's rooftop deck, with its panoramic river view.

The hotel manager said at check-in that the Elliott had been a rundown property until about 10 years ago, when investors transformed it into a boutique hotel with heated bathroom floors and a wine bar in the lobby. It wasn't Chicago, but it wasn't bad, Williams thought.

Soon he and his partner were joined by an agent from the Portland office who looked somewhat embarrassed.

"I thought you boys would like this," the man said, handing Williams an envelope. "Came in the mail days ago. We didn't realize the connection until this morning."

Williams gave the man a look of exasperation. Failing to make timely connections in vital cases was something of an FBI curse.

He pulled the pages out and unfolded them. It began with these words: "Dear Investigators: It's a rescue, not a kidnapping, if the baby was previously stolen from its mother. Please allow me to explain."

The investigator excused his Portland colleague and sat down in a lounge chair next to a fire pit spitting flames. It was nearly May and there was still a chill in the late-afternoon air.

As Bellows paced, Williams read the typed statement from "Anonymous." When he was finished, he knew his instincts about the case had been correct.

"Our mystery man," he said. "First he calls the cops. Now he's a whistleblower."

"You're kidding me," Bellows said, stopping in his tracks.

"This is a strange one," the senior agent said. "Get the team together. We have work to do."

23

Bud found an Alaska station on the FM radio, heard an old rock song and instantly felt better.

"Lord, I was born a ramblin' man," he sang, cranking up the volume until the door speakers pulsed.

"When it's time for leavin,' I hope you'll understand, that I was born a ramblin' man."

It was high noon and Bud was making good time. As he entered what looked like a long straightaway, he sat back and relaxed a bit. He'd be in Anchorage in a few days.

There had been no police roadblocks and, more importantly, no big black pickups from Idaho. Maybe the man hunting him had no idea where he was headed. Maybe the law wasn't after him this far north in British Columbia.

Just maybe, he could live his Kodiak dream.

He smiled at the thought of it. The Allman Brothers were in their final chorus and he joined in.

"I was born a ramblin' man!"

—

Withers peered through his scope and caught a glimpse of the purple Jeep headed directly toward him. Just as he had predicted.

"Gotcha."

The hunter readied the Springfield, the weapon his father, the cattleman, had handed down to him. Over the years, it had become his trusted partner, helping him rid his land of thieving wolves and bag trophy bucks.

Now the rifle was about to bring him something far better – long overdue justice.

He ran his hand over the stock, admiring its dark beauty, its velvety finish. He caressed it like a woman then put one eye to the scope.

At less than a mile out, he could see Baker in the driver's seat, happily rocking back and forth.

The bastard is singing!

The sheriff's face flushed with fury and he had to command himself to breathe deeply and control his emotions.

Baker was now less than 900 yards away, coming right to him.

It was a challenging shot, through a windshield on a moving vehicle.

But the .30-06 was no ordinary gun. It packed a powerful punch, capable of dropping a charging moose with a single shot.

He calmly chambered one of the large bullets and wedged the rifle butt under his right shoulder. His index finger tickled the trigger.

The target was now just 200 yards from the kill spot. He could hear the Jeep's engine, the sound the knobby tires were making on the surface of the highway.

Steady.

Baker's face now filled the sight.

He'd wipe that grin off that sonofabitch's face. His finger began squeezing the trigger …

"Hey!"

A voice from behind startled the old sheriff.

"What are you doing with that gun! Step away with your hands up!"

Withers winced as the Jeep barreled by, headed north. He had been so close. So very close. But there would be another opportunity, he knew. He had no intention of giving up.

He straightened, hands in the air as he was told. When he turned, he saw an officer aiming a pistol at him. His Royal Canadian Mounted Police car was parked on the other side of the hill. Withers hadn't noticed.

"Just doing some hunting, officer," Wither said, regaining his cool.

"Hunting? Across a highway? Did you not see that Jeep? You could have killed someone."

That was the plan, until you got in the way.

"No, I was just scoping a moose. I lost it in the trees."

"Let's see some identification," the Mountie said, still skeptical.

Withers pulled a driver's license that had his retired law enforcement status on it and the Canadian's officer's attitude instantly changed.

"You're an ex-cop?"

Withers nodded. "Former sheriff down in Idaho. Before that I did highway enforcement, like you. Before that, the Army."

"Sorry to yell at you, sir. From a distance, it looked like you were aiming at that vehicle. I hope you understand."

"Certainly. I appreciate your vigilance. Am I free to go?"

The Mountie tipped his wide-brimmed hat. "Yes, sir. Have a nice day."

Before he got in his cruiser, he yelled up the hill, "Good elk hunting about thirty miles northeast of here, in Bridal Meadow. They come down to drink."

Withers nodded and watched as the patrol car disappeared. Cursing, he nestled the unused Springfield in its case.

He climbed in the Ford and took a few deep breaths to steady his breathing.

Then he headed north.

———

Sweet called the place Bud named, but the man who answered just said, "What can I do for you?"

"Is this Frontier Ridge? The store?"

"That's right."

"I'm a friend of Bud Baker and he said I could leave a message for him," the reporter said.

"He's not here."

"No, I just want to leave a message."

"Why would you want to do that when he's not here? Hasn't been here for many years. Seems like a waste of time, son."

"He's heading there now and he doesn't have a phone. He said if I had some important news for him, I could call and leave a message. Can I leave a message with you?"

Sully Sullivan was not keen on doing other people favors. He barely knew this Baker and, besides, he had a general store to run.

At nearly 90, with a bad heart and a back that perpetually ached, he should have retired a long time ago. But then he figured not working was something of a death sentence also. Either way, he had it covered with a funeral package paid in full.

In a sudden burst of clarity, the shopkeeper remembered that his old friend Elmore, God rest his soul, had sold Baker his cabin and thought he was a decent enough fellow — for an outlaw.

That part was no surprise. The Alaska woods were thick with people either searching for or escaping from something.

"*Hello?* Are you still there?"

"Yeah, yeah, I'm here," Sullivan groused, grabbing a pen. "Okay, what's this message that's so important I have to write it down?"

"Just tell him that the man tracking him is the former Owyhee County sheriff, a man named Frank Withers."

"Sheriff Withers. Got it."

"And please add this: Withers' son was the deputy killed in the shootout. He'll know what that means."

Sullivan scribbled the information down on a scrap of paper, causing his gnarled fingers to ache.

"I've got the arthritis. Hurts like the dickens sometimes. Anything else I have to write down?"

Sweet ignored the old man's protestations. This warning was of vital importance.

"Yeah, tell him his life is in danger. Please say it's from Roger Sweet. That's me. I really appreciate it. What's your name?"

"I'm Sully, the owner. I'll see he gets the message – if he makes it here."

"If you see an older man with a cowboy hat in a black pickup truck from Idaho, watch out. He's out of his mind."

"Sounds like this Baker's in some trouble."

"Yeah," Sweet said. "And then some."

24

At 77 mph, it was hard for Bud to see things on the side of the road with any clarity. Objects passed by quickly, in a blur – if he saw them at all.

But with the Jeep's radio blaring and himself in mid-song, he still caught two disturbing glimpses on the highway in western British Columbia.

The first was the sudden appearance of the back end of a patrol car that caused him to immediately take his foot off the gas, fearing a speed trap that could lead to his capture.

The second was the image in the rear-view mirror of a vehicle on top of a knoll, near the police cruiser, that very much looked like a large black pickup.

Bud wasn't paranoid about being hunted at this point. He knew with absolute certainty he was. But what was the pickup cowboy doing with Canadian police? Were they working together to take him in, dead or alive?

"Fuck me!" he yelled, pounding his fists against the steering wheel. His oasis of calm had been short-lived.

It seemed obvious that the pickup was on the hill because it offered a perfect sniper's vantage point. So why didn't the bastard take the damn shot?

Maybe he's just toying with me. Taking his time.

He knew there was still a long way to go, a looping northwesterly hook through hundreds of miles of wilderness, just to get to Anchorage. With the hunter seemingly always one step ahead, Bud feared there would be plenty of opportunities for an ambush along the route.

Unless, of course, he radically changed the route.

He glanced at the crumpled map laid out across the passenger seat and saw something that gave him hope: a small airport less than a hundred miles ahead, outside of Whitehorse in the Yukon Territory.

A new plan started taking shape.

There was no way, as a fugitive without a phony ID, that he could take a commercial flight. But he did have plenty of cash thanks to the Astoria baby-peddlers.

If he could get to the airfield and persuade a private pilot to fly him to Kodiak, there was a chance he could escape his highway-bound pursuers – possibly even for good.

He had been on the verge of a panic attack only moments ago. Now he leaned back and allowed himself a nervous smile.

"I can be persuasive," said the ex-convict who had managed to sway a few federal judges and juries. "Let's try Door No. 2."

———

Bud was happy to still be alive when he arrived at the small airport.

Built by the government during World War II for the Royal Canadian Air Force, it now served the far-flung territory as a civilian airport, offering three modest runways and limited commercial service.

A number of air charter operators and bush pilots used the facility. Looking around, Bud also saw a few water bombers ready to take flight and fight forest fires.

Skirting the main terminal, Bud steered the Jeep around to where the charters were located and parked outside the hangar for Archer Air Service. He scaled a 6-foot-high, chain-link security fence marked "Authorized Personnel Only" and headed onto the tarmac.

Spotting a pilot adjusting the propeller on a single-engine Cessna 172 Skyhawk, Bud approached with a smile.

"Is that your plane?" he asked.

The man with the wrench didn't bother turning around.

"Nobody's allowed out here. Talk to the lady inside if you want to book a charter."

"I was hoping to cut out the middleman – or middle lady, I suppose. I have a special request, but I'll make it worth your time."

With that bait cast, the pilot turned to face Bud. He was in his late 20s but looked much older, with a prematurely receding hair line and a ruddy complexion, cheeks streaked with grease.

"Oh yeah?"

"Yeah. Whatever your standard rate is, I'll triple it."

"You don't look rich to me."

"I'm not, but I have to get to Kodiak and I think you're just the man to do it. Name your price."

"Kodiak? Are you crazy? We don't fly that far. Take a commercial flight. There's one leaving for Anchorage in a couple of hours."

Bud sighed.

"I can't explain, but that's not possible. Look, I'll toss in that Jeep over there."

"The Laredo?" the pilot said, staring at the shiny vehicle parked on the other side of the fence. "The purple one?"

"That's the one."

"Man, that's a nice ride. You really *do* need to get to Kodiak."

"I really do. I'll pay you $5,000 cash for the flight, plus the Jeep. Sound fair?"

The pilot gave Bud a gap-toothed smile.

"Mister, it's a deal. I don't know what you're into or who may be after you, but I'll get you where you need to be."

They shook hands. It would be a costly trip, but well worth the price, Bud thought. At any moment a pickup driven by a crazed cowboy could arrive at the airfield. Bullets would fly.

"How soon can we take off?"

"Soon as I clean up and tell Margie that I'll be gone the next two days. You lucked out on the weather, pal – just had a storm pass through."

Wishing he still had his pistol, Bud grabbed his cash-filled bag and stuffed a few clothes inside. He left the keys in the glove box. Then he walked up the plane's short metal stairs to the cabin and took a seat.

Less than 30 minutes later, the Cessna, white with thick red stripes, was taxiing on the smallest of the airport's runways. Bud was close enough to the cockpit to hear the tower chatter in the pilot's headset, giving him approval to take off.

As the plane rose above the airport, Bud found himself scanning the roads for his hunter's hulking vehicle. He didn't see anything and breathed a little easier.

"Mind if I ask what business you've got in Kodiak?" the pilot asked after the Skyhawk reached cruising altitude. "Name's Rusty, by the way. Rusty Parker."

"No business," the weary passenger replied without giving his name. "I'm gonna live there, free as can be."

"Well, mister, I want to thank you for crossing my path. Now I can sell my old truck and use your cash to buy an engagement ring."

"Best of luck. I don't think I'm cut out for marriage."

"Why's that?"

"Too trusting."

Both men laughed.

Bud excused himself and closed his eyes. He was exhausted and hadn't slept in the past 24 hours.

Soon, he hoped, he'd be home.

25

Just four blocks off The Strip, one of the planet's busiest tourist meccas, it was strangely quiet.

Jessie and Jo Jo had rented a furnished two-bedroom cottage in a tree-lined, middle-class neighborhood. The house also had an office, which they immediately turned into a nursery, installing a crib and converting a desk into a changing table, its drawers stuffed with wipes, powder and diapers.

The fugitive sisters were starting over in almost every way. It began with changing their names, with Jessie choosing Ann Thompson and Jo Jo picking Margret Hawthorne.

That they began referring to themselves collectively as Ann-Margret was a private joke.

Jessie dyed her hair dark brown, while Jo Jo, refusing to change her scarlet locks, wore a black wig when she ventured out, which wasn't often since she was terrified of being swept up by federal agents.

At night, when the neon glow from the grand, casino-lined boulevard was visible from her bedroom window, Jo Jo thought pensively about Bud and his passion for the Northern Lights.

I hope you're safe.

Please don't hate me.

I'm sorry.

While Jo Jo struggled, Jessie thrived.

She named her son Patrick Lee, after a great-grandfather, and immediately began spoiling him with all kinds of toys and a mobile above his bed that played "Twinkle, Twinkle Little Star" and projected celestial images on the ceiling.

The baby was crawling now, a feat that was nearly discovered too late, with Patrick coming perilously close to falling off the changing table. The chubby tot would smile and stare dreamily into his mother's eyes as she fed him bottles of formula. She'd stare back, just as dreamily.

For Jessie, it was a miracle she was nearly denied. She would always be grateful to Bud for returning her son to her. For giving her this chance.

In exchange, she continued to stay sober. She joined a Narcotics Anonymous group, which were plentiful in the gambler's paradise. Every day that passed without a needle in her arm was a step closer to being truly alive.

She sold the Subaru for cash, with the sisters agreeing to walk or take the bus instead of driving – just to be safe.

Jessie landed a waitressing job at a fancy steakhouse. On her second day on the job she was promoted to hostess, based largely on her sunny disposition and ready smile. It felt good to be upbeat again, she thought.

Jo Jo, though, was miserable.

Unable emotionally to look for a job, she took care of the baby when her sister worked. Most of the time she stayed indoors, afraid to take Patrick out in the stroller for fear of being caught.

Las Vegas wasn't her kind of place, she quickly realized. The monument to decadent extravagance rose in the middle of a desert – too far from the ocean she loved.

She envied Bud's natural paradise and thought about how lovely it must be in springtime. She wrote him several long letters, begging for his forgiveness, but tore them all up.

Even if she had the nerve to mail them, she had no address. She didn't even have a phone number. All she knew was a place: A log cabin by a small lake in the woods near Kodiak.

Jo Jo did her best to hide her gloom from her younger sister, who had seemingly overnight transformed from recovering addict to giddy mom, full of passion and promise.

But like any loving sibling, Jessie knew.

"Sis, you need to get out more," she said one evening. "We've been here four days, the weather's fantastic, and you've only been to the supermarket and back. *Once*."

"I'm a coward, I guess."

"Hah! No one would ever accuse you of that. You're the strongest person I know – have ever known."

"Not anymore."

Jessie sat next to Jo Jo on the couch and began bouncing Patrick on her knees.

"I think if you get a job, even something part-time, it would help."

"I'm not ready."

"For what, exactly? For moving on with your life here, or moving on without him?"

Jo Jo didn't answer. She had refused to rain on her sister's resurgence, and yet Jessie still felt her despair.

More than that, she had evidence.

A few days earlier a book had arrived at the house via Amazon addressed to Margret Hawthorne.

Jessie found it under her sister's bed while retrieving one of Patrick's errant plastic balls.

It was a travel guide to Alaska.

26

As Bud flew across the Gulf of Alaska, the FBI learned his name.

Federal agents visited the Clatsop County Jail, where Josephine Summers had worked with low-level drug offenders and the shelter in the church where she had aided the homeless. The investigators sifted through records at both places, questioned a few people, and struck gold.

The social worker, they soon discovered, had bailed out a man named Wallace Baker after he'd been arrested for assault. She also found him a job and a place to live.

Clearly, Summers had taken a special interest in Baker, who had recently been released from prison in Boise. He had a history of armed robbery and served 25 years behind bars, but that was only part of the story.

Baker had become a jailhouse lawyer credited with reforming the Idaho prison system, and the governor, eager to rid himself of a pest, ordered him released.

That explained a few things, Williams thought, including the five-page statement sent to the bureau anonymously. In his 36-year career, it was the most detailed tip about an alleged criminal enterprise he'd ever received.

Based on that and the obviously forged adoption papers, Williams obtained a warrant and returned to Little Angels. The FBI team seized the agency's business records, along with all of the employees' cell phones and computers.

At the same time, agents scoured Krump's upscale Astoria home for evidence, filling several large boxes.

When the director angrily demanded an explanation, Williams was happy to oblige.

"We have opened a trafficking investigation," he told her.

"Trafficking? In *what*?"

"Babies, Mrs. Krump," he said. "Babies."

"That's preposterous! We find unwanted babies good, loving homes. We are faith-based. We serve a higher purpose."

"Some of the babies you placed weren't 'unwanted,' were they?" the agent said, dark eyes flashing. "Jessie Summers' child, for instance."

"I don't know what you're talking about. She's a drug addict – she has zero credibility."

"I suggest you find yourself an experienced defense lawyer. You'll need one."

He reached in the pocket of his suit and handed the woman his business card. "You can give him that."

If the seized records yielded evidence supporting the anonymous allegations Baker and the sisters likely had made in the letter to the FBI, Williams could bring a case before a federal grand jury. Human trafficking, criminal conspiracy, forgery, falsification of records – a menu of potential crimes was on the table.

And if the claims of involvement in the scheme by Astoria city and police officials were also true, the investigation could mushroom into a major scandal.

There was a kidnapper on the run to deal with, but the special agent now had a good idea where his prime suspect was headed.

The convict has been released from the penitentiary on several stringent conditions, one of which was that he go to a forested island in Alaska, where a man had volunteered to be his sponsor.

"You think he went to Kodiak with the sisters and the baby?" Bellows asked his partner at the Elliott. They were back on the brick-walled hotel's breezy rooftop deck, which Williams found conducive to his sleuthing.

"Probably just Baker and the girlfriend. My hunch is they planned to split up, with the younger sister and baby headed in a different direction."

"The bulletin is for a man and a baby. Should we change that?"

"Not just yet. We need to focus on Baker. He's the key. I think he planned everything."

"What about Josephine Summers?"

"I think she put the plan in motion by recruiting Baker, but after reading his statement I'm pretty sure he planned every detail of the kidnapping."

"He must know we'll come looking for him in Kodiak."

"No doubt. I think he's just buying time, hoping we'll prove his claims for him."

The men paused on their perch to watch a pilot boat guide a massive freighter into the harbor. Bellows searched his partner's face. He was often hard to read.

"If we arrest him, he's going back to prison for the rest of his life."

"Yeah," Williams said with a trace of sympathy. "I think he was trying to do the right thing – get the baby back, expose that adoption center. Christ, he even called police about the couple in the basement. Who does that when they're on the run?"

"But he tied them up at gunpoint."

"Yes, he did. A blast from his past. Well, I guess we'll deal with that when we catch him."

"What's going to happen to the baby? You can't take it away from its birth mother, right? Not again."

William shrugged.

"We'll let a judge decide. There's a moral thing to do, and a legal thing to do. They don't always agree."

The veteran agent looked at his watch and saw it was later in the evening than he thought.

"Have you ever been to Alaska, Ron? I hear it's lovely this time of year."

———

Bud looked out his porthole window with great interest as Rusty Parker flew a sloppy circle around richly forested Kodiak Island before touching down.

He could see tourist-beckoning float planes, Coast Guard ships and an enormous armada of fishing boats.

The Cessna landed with a couple of hops. Parker steered the plane to an area away from the lone terminal.

"I figure you may want to avoid security," the pilot told his only passenger.

"Right. I'll be walking from here into town."

"I really hope you make it. You seem like a nice guy."

"There's a slim chance of success, but it's all I've got."

Bud had counted out $5,000 in hundred-dollar bills and handed the stack to Parker, who whistled at the windfall that could push him closer to matrimony.

"Please tell me it's not mob money," the pilot said.

"It's not mob money. Or drug money."

A righteous crime.

"The keys to the Jeep are in the glove box," the bushy-haired outlaw said. "Thanks for the ride."

The men embraced and Bud slung his knapsack over a shoulder and stepped out onto the tarmac.

"Good luck!" Parker shouted.

Bud gave him a two-fingered salute and slipped between a storage area and a hangar, disappearing into some spindly pines.

It took him less than an hour of walking to reach the heart of downtown Kodiak, which had changed a lot in 25 years, with the addition of a brewery and a few resort hotels and day spas.

But he found Frontier Ridge General Store right away.

It had the same gray, cedar-shingle exterior, only more weathered. There was also the same carved, politically incorrect Indian by the front door and the same wooden bench under the front windows.

Bud stepped inside. The lights were on but there were no signs of anyone.

"Hello?"

Bud heard banging and rustling sounds from a storage room.

"Just a minute!"

Moments later, Sullivan emerged, wiping off his wrinkled brow with the handkerchief that seemed to always be in his hand. He was breathing hard when he reached the counter.

"Do I know you?" he asked, straightening his bowtie and squinting at Bud like a far-sighted art appraiser. "Memory ain't what it used to be."

"Bud Baker. Been gone a long time."

"Baker," the old man repeated, buying time for his mind to find the right gear. "The outlaw!"

Bud cringed. "Like I said, it was a long time ago."

"Well, you're alive, so that tells me something. An outlaw who doesn't die is either smart or lucky."

"Lucky, I guess."

He would have protested against being labeled an outlaw, but he was, in fact, a baby-napping fugitive.

"So, what are you running from now? The law or a woman?" In Sullivan's mind, those were the only two logical choices.

"I'm not running. I'm putting down roots. I've come to reclaim a cabin in the woods and live off the land as best I can."

"Baker. Yeah, I remember you a little better now. You bought Elmore's old place, on the ridge by the lake. Been boarded up for years. Dunno if any pests have broken in. You'll find out soon enough."

Bud grunted. He'd have to find the strength to fix the old place up on his own – without a certain beautiful but treacherous redhead.

"Heading there today. Gonna need a lot of supplies."

Sullivan's tired eyes brightened. "Well, son, you came to the right place. Let's get to work."

Bud laughed as the shopkeeper shuffled out into the store with a large cardboard box in each hand and began tossing in items. He loaded up a bag of rags, cleaning fluids of various kinds, sponges, a campfire-style coffee pot and matches as a start.

By the time they were done, five boxes were filled. On the side leaned an axe, a broom and a mop with a bucket.

"Now let's get you something to shoot with," Sullivan said with a bit of excitement.

They walked over to the guns-and-ammo section of the store and he handed Bud a shotgun and a box of shells.

"This won't stop a bear, but it'll take down a deer and put a burglar in the ground," the owner said with a wink.

The wink made Bud think of his pal Harry. He held the pump-action Remington 870, admiring its no-frills, sleek design.

"Nice gun."

"It won't fail you, son. Just point and shoot."

"Point and shoot. Got it."

Seeing how big the pile of supplies was getting, he posed a question.

"Hey, can I borrow one of your trucks out back? I had to get rid of my Jeep."

Sullivan chortled in a phlegmy way that made him dab his cracked lips with the handkerchief.

"Hah. Don't think you can carry all this for five miles? Go ahead and load up the old Chevy in back. Keys are in it. Watch the ruts, just had the tranny fixed."

"Will do," Bud said, grabbing one of the overloaded boxes.

"I'll put everything on your tab. Don't need to keep you waiting. I'm a little slow with the calculating these days."

"I've got money, don't worry."

"Oh, I ain't worried. If you don't pay, you'll be working it off right here. I can use the help."

Bud put the supplies into the rusted bed of the pickup and climbed in. As the truck sprang to life, he saw Sullivan, hunched over, hustling toward him.

"Dang!" he said as he reached the Chevy, taking gulps of air. "Forgot to give you something."

"What's that?"

"Got a message for you. From a friend of yours."

He handed Bud a note through the window.

The writing was shaky and difficult to read, but it said: "Sheriff Withers from Idaho coming for you. Obsessed. Revenge. Be careful. Sweet."

"That's it?"

"That's the gist of it. I wrote it down right after he called, which is a good thing. Memory's not what it used to be."

He slapped the roof of the pickup and shuffled back into the store, pleased with himself for delivering the note.

Bud sat in the truck for a while, digesting the new information.

He remembered the old sheriff. His son died in the shootout, 25 years earlier, that resulted in Bud's capture.

It suddenly occurred to him that the man on his tail wasn't a hired gun at all. It was the angry person in the front row at his parole hearing wearing the Stetson.

If Sweet was right, Bud knew the hunter wouldn't stop. Not until he was dead.

But as the truck labored up the hill, over narrow dirt roads and through forest so thick it blotted out the sun, the assassin's target felt oddly at ease.

He has to find me first.

And if he does, I'll be ready.

27

The resplendent log cabin Bud admired in his youth was no longer evident.

His heart sank as he approached the front steps. Only his newfound confidence as a home renovator kept him moving forward.

The once-charming stone path leading to the front of the cabin looked like it had been struck by mortar shells. The treads on the stairs were either cracked, rotting or both. The low roof over the wide porch sagged in the middle. The brick chimney looked in serious need of new mortar.

He grabbed a claw hammer and used it pry off the plywood covering the windows and was relieved to find the glass and frames intact.

Stepping carefully to avoid falling through the stair boards, Bud tied a red-and-white scarf around his neck, pulled it over his nose like a bandit and opened the door.

He expected to find it empty inside, but there was some rustic wooden furniture covered by white sheets. Thrown in by ol' Elmore as part of the deal, he supposed.

Thick cobwebs hung in every corner, and as he walked, clouds of dust rose. He heard a field mouse squeak from somewhere and cursed.

The stone fireplace and its oak mantel were in decent shape, he noticed, which was good because he intended to light a fire that evening after some vigorous cleaning.

There were a few pots and pans in the kitchen cupboards, and also some plates and a few ceramic cups, but the cabinets were otherwise empty. There was a small fridge and a sink but no other modern conveniences.

In the bedroom was an old brass bed frame and a four-drawer cedar dresser. He stepped into the adjoining bathroom, relieved to find it surprisingly intact. A claw-foot tub had become home to one of the largest spiders he'd ever seen, the toilet tank had a cracked lid and the wooden medicine cabinet lacked a door, but he had expected worse.

Bud found the main water valve and gave it a few turns. He was relieved to see liquid start to flow in the kitchen sink — brown at first, then yellow and finally clear. He found the circuit box and flicked the main power breaker on.

"Oh yeah!" he shouted gleefully as the fridge began to hum. "We're in business!"

Bud moved all the stuff from the pickup into the house and found the bottle of dark Jamaican rum Sullivan had slipped in. He took a long drink and felt the liquor warming his gut.

Then he opened the door and as many windows as he could and started sweeping.

He made a mental note to buy a radio when he was next in town. Music always made the work go faster.

Two hours later, the floors and windows had been cleaned, the spider webs eradicated. Bud pulled the sheets off the furniture and admired a lounge chair built out of cedar logs. He poked the cushion with a finger and was surprised by its firmness.

He spent another hour installing new treads on the front steps, then decided to gather some firewood.

His new axe slung over his shoulder, he ventured into a stand of pines and began pulling some thick branches into a pile for easy chopping. Then he caught a glimpse of a vivid blue.

His father's lake.

When he drew closer his pulse quickened. The old fishing pier, long and narrow, was still standing, extending some fifty feet into the water.

He walked the length of it and sat on the edge. In the reflection off the water he saw a man and a young boy.

———

"This is the life, Buddy."

Brad Baker stretched his arms to the pure-blue sky and smiled at his son. They were sitting on the pier on a calm summer afternoon.

Baker grabbed a fishing rod and showed Buddy the hook.

"We'll put some bait on that, then a hungry fish will come along and bite it. That's when we reel it in, Buddy. Catch our dinner."

He put a wriggling worm on the hook and stood up to give it a cast. There was a small splash and Buddy watched, wide-eyed, as a red plastic float bobbed on the surface of the lake about 30 yards away.

"Now hold this pole between your legs and slowly reel in the line, like this," Baker said, turning the handle for the 10-year-old. "Go very slow. We'll know if the fish are biting today pretty soon."

Baker took a drink from a bottle of beer and cast his own line.

"Dad, is this our lake?"

"No Buddy, we're just borrowing it for a day."

"I like it here."

"I know, pal. I like it, too."

"Can we live here?"

The father laughed. "I think Elmore up there wouldn't like that. But we can sure visit from time to time."

"How did you find this place? I mean, the first time."

"I was hunting elk with some friends the day I first saw it, up on that ridge over there. I looked down and saw a sliver of blue and thought it was one of the most beautiful things I'd ever seen."

Buddy smiled. He liked it when his dad was enthralled about something – from sports on TV to the shine on his car.

"Dad?"

"Yes?"

"Why don't you take Mom here?"

The look on Baker's face changed, losing some of its bliss, but his son was too young to notice.

"Sometimes, a man just has to be alone. To figure things out. That's why, son."

"What are you figuring out?"

"My life, my future," he said, then tousled Buddy's curly hair. "Grownup stuff."

"I love you, Dad."

"Love you, too."

"I'm glad you're not alone."

Buddy hugged his father, and then the boy shrieked as his line tightened, nearly pulling the pole from his little hands.

His father got behind him and they both pulled.

When a trout breached the lake's glassy surface, its tail swishing, Baker shouted, "You got one, Buddy! A real beauty!"

Together, they reeled in their prize.

———

Tears welled in Bud's eyes and the vision disappeared as if washed away.

His bitter childhood memories, the ones scratched into his psyche after the fishing trip, were not so easily dismissed. Not since the dam holding them back burst.

When he was 10 or 11 years old, life couldn't be better. At home in Medford, he had a shoebox full of army men and a train set to play with. He was the smartest kid in his classes.

His mother, an aspiring artist with a home studio in which to harness her inspiration, would always be waiting for Buddy after school with a hug.

But then, one day, his father vanished.

Brad Baker gave his wife a peck on the cheek at 7:30 that morning, the time he'd usually head to work managing a print shop. He got in the Buick and never returned.

Emily Baker, frantic, reported her husband missing late that night. She gave deputies a recent photograph and they notified all units, but they couldn't find a trace of him.

The print shop said he quit weeks earlier. The Buick was found parked at a train station about 50 miles away. There was no note or any sign of foul play.

As the days passed, Bud, the only child, witnessed up close his mother's emotional torment. One day she'd put up a brave front, the next she'd break down in shoulder-heaving sobs.

"I thought we were happy," she'd often say. "I thought we were happy."

Bud comforted her as well as a 12-year-old could, but his mother's breakdown appeared to have no bottom. Soon, she began drowning her sorrows. When her son took out the garbage, he'd hear the gin bottles clanking.

She stopped painting and began inviting strange men to the house. Some of them treated her badly. Even the thickest makeup couldn't hide the bruises. When she left the house, she'd wear a headscarf and dark sunglasses.

By then Bud had become a rebellious teenager. He'd steal money from the men sleeping with his mom and smoke pot with his friends. He'd stay out all night, skip school, only to find his mother slumped over the kitchen table fast asleep, a cigarette still smoldering between her fingers. He'd put the butt in the ashtray and check the fridge, only to find it empty.

He wanted to leave and never come back, but that was exactly what his father had done.

Instead, Bud disappeared gradually. When he turned 16, he moved out of the house and began living on his own, working odd jobs. When he fell into crime, his absences grew longer and longer.

Every Christmas he'd show up with a gift for his mother, who looked even more frail with every passing year. He'd make up some lie about some important job he had, in some big city he'd never been to.

"Please don't stay away so long, Buddy," she would say.

"I won't, Ma," he'd answer.

After a day or two, he'd slip away.

Decades later, he was still slipping away.

Cursing himself for being such a softie, Bud looked across the lake and saw a large buck with kingly antlers watching him, welcoming him to the neighborhood.

"Spread the news, big fella! Bud's back!" he called out, causing an echo that prompted the buck to leap into the brush.

As the sun sunk low, the sky turned a pastel orange streaked with blue. The outlaw admired the artistry above with a touch of sadness.

It was a moment best shared and he sat alone.

28

Jo Jo paced the living room, Patrick cooing in her arms.

She traced circles until her legs ached and the baby dozed, but her mind was always someplace else. Someplace far away.

One day, after putting Patrick down in his crib, she turned to see Jessie watching from the hall.

"Sis, we need to talk," she said.

They sat on the couch and Jessie patted her big sister's knee in a comforting way.

"JJ, I know you're hurting, but you have to stop punishing yourself. We're here, we're safe. It's time to start over."

"I don't want to start over."

"I know, but you have no choice. The past is behind us."

Jo Jo sighed so deeply her body shook.

"It doesn't have to be," she said.

"Sis, he's gone. He's in the wilds of Alaska now, off the grid or whatever. And if you show up – if you somehow are able to find him – he'd tell you to go to hell. You need to move on with your life – here, with me and Pat."

"I love him, Jessie. More than any man I've ever known."

"But how do you know he still loves you?"

"I should have told him I was going with you. Explained the situation. He would have understood. He would have waited for me."

It was Jessie's turn to sigh.

"You don't need to be here, sis," she said. "I know you don't like Vegas. You're an ocean girl. Besides, I'm doing fine."

"I know."

"You can stop being my private social worker. I have my baby now. I won't relapse, no goddamn way."

"I'm so proud of you, Jess."

There was a long silence as they both struggled to find the right words.

"Go to him. Get your answers," Jessie said finally.

"I want to. I want to so badly."

"Do it then."

"But who'll take care of the baby?"

"Mrs. Sanchez next door has offered a half-dozen times. I'll take her up on it. Or I'll find a daycare."

"Sis ..."

"Go!" Jessie said firmly. Suddenly she was the one in charge. "I'm tired of you pacing around the house. You're wearing out the new rug."

"Do you really mean it?"

"Go to Alaska. Get answers. It's the only way, I suppose. He's a good man, despite, you know, the time when he wasn't.

"Maybe you're right. Maybe he misses you as much as you miss him. It's like a cheesy rom-com, except with fugitives and stuff."

Jo Jo hugged her sister tightly. She smiled and for the first time in days, her face lit up, showing her true beauty.

"I love you," she said.

"Just be careful. Don't get yourself arrested. I don't like jails. I won't visit you."

"Good to know," the older sister said with a pretend scowl, before disappearing into her bedroom.

Moments later, she called out: "How much should I pack?"

29

Bud's return to Kodiak wasn't exactly what he'd imagined.

While he was a free man in the great outdoors, just like he'd dreamed for countless nights in his prison cell, there was a catch.

His cherished freedom could end at any moment. He was a wanted and hunted man, and he knew that eventually he'd be found. Most likely at gunpoint.

So, every trip to town came with a knot in his stomach. He'd been back for three days and hadn't hit a single bar, though he thirsted for both beer and company. It just seemed way too risky.

But there was one thing he absolutely, positively had to have. A fishing rod.

"Forgot something," he told Sullivan as he put the rod and tackle on the counter.

"Seems more like you remembered something," the shopkeeper said, smiling. "Elmore told me the story about you and your pa."

"Yeah, well, thought I'd try a little fishing tomorrow."

"That's the spirit, son. Enjoy the time you've got left."

Bud thought the old geezer was talking about himself, but Sullivan added: "If they gun you down, I'm gonna name that lake after you: Baker Lake."

"Thanks. Doesn't that oversized pond already have a name?"

"Not that I remember, but …"

"I know, your memory is really bad these days."

Bud thanked the octogenarian and returned home, relieved as always not to see any black pickups from out of state.

It was sunset when he finished his bowl of homemade venison stew and decided to take a walk. Naturally, he ended up at the lake. An eagle soared overhead. Several spotted deer were taking a drink on the opposite shore.

He heard a rustling sound and turned around. What he saw took his breath away.

A mermaid.

Standing on the grassy path by the pier.

With scarlet hair and glowing green eyes.

"Hello Bud," she said.

———

As the outlaw stood on the pier, dumbstruck, Jo Jo smiled.

"I knew I'd find you here," she said. "On your dock of the lake."

"What are you doing here? How did you find me?"

"A very nice man named Sully gave me directions. He said you could use a hand."

She walked over and wrapped her arms tightly around him. Her embrace lasted more than a minute, but his arms hung limp.

"I'm so sorry, Bud. I love you and I miss you so much," she said. "I'll never hurt you again, I promise."

Bud didn't know whether he could believe her.

"Why didn't you just tell me you needed to go with Jessie? Why didn't you just say goodbye?"

"I didn't know until that night. I panicked. I thought about her being on the run with the baby, and I convinced myself she needed my help. Turns out, I was wrong. She's stronger than I ever knew."

"After what you did, you shouldn't have come here. You should have stayed in Vegas."

"I was there four days and I just had to leave. Darling, I knew I had to be with you."

Bud said nothing.

She laid her hands on his shoulders and looked into his eyes.

A tear rolled down her soft white cheek and Bud brushed it away.

"Do you think I'm a bad person?" she asked.

"No. Never."

"I wrote you long letters asking you to forgive me, but I thought I'd just ask you in person. Will you?"

Bud turned to the lake and wiped away a tear of his own.

"I was angry at first when you disappeared. Then I was sad. I thought I'd lost you forever. But now, seeing you here, I feel happy. Is that love?"

Jo Jo hugged him from behind, resting her head against his back. "Yes, darling, that's love."

He pulled her to him and kissed her warm lips.

It was getting cold and she was only wearing a sweater. He took her hand and led her to the cabin, stopping to grab an armload of his freshly chopped firewood.

"It's a work in progress," he said as he opened the door.

Jo Jo spun in a slow-motion circle, drinking it all in.

"It's so lovely. Better than you described."

Bud suddenly felt euphoric. The woman he loved had returned. It was as close to believing in magic that he'd ever come.

He'd wait until morning to tell her an assassin was coming.

30

The ferry to Kodiak Island was full of cars and people, most of them tourists eager to do some fishing and hunting.

Withers ignored them all.

The hunter leaned on the steel railing ringing the top deck, hat pulled tight against the wind, Ray-Bans reflecting the afternoon sun peeking through gray-tinged clouds. He felt the vibrations of the boat as it began to slow a half-mile from the dock.

I'm coming for you, criminal.

Baker was out there, somewhere in the woods, and he would find him. His tracking prowess had never failed him. And even though he was an older man now, he remained cool and confident. There were some skills you didn't lose with age.

The former sheriff also knew his decades-long nightmare would soon be over. Maybe today. Two days max.

He'd find Baker and kill him, only this time the reckoning would not come from a bullet fired from a safe distance. No, this time he'd exact his revenge up close, looking his tormentor in the eyes.

The lawman would stand over Baker, watch his life drain away in a puddle of blood, and smile.

Standing on the deck, the cold ocean spray spritzing his weathered face, Withers thought about his wife and son. He was doing this for them. So they could rest in peace.

It was selfless, really. His own life mattered little. He was old and prepared to die.

Before he went after Baker he'd had to take care of a few things. One had been to update his will. Another had been to secure a gravesite at the rural cemetery next to Molly's.

Now that his affairs were in order, he was free to avenge what had been taken from him.

Johnny and Molly.

———

Molly Ann Caruso was a tranquil woman with simple dreams who fell for a rugged lawman with chiseled features and brilliant blue eyes. She thought he looked like a movie star.

When they married and he was gone many nights chasing bad guys on the high desert plains of southwest Idaho, she accepted it as part of the bargain. She tried not to think about the dangers her husband faced – only that he'd soon return and their happy life together would resume.

They ran a small black Angus ranch inherited from his father and most of the work managing the house and cattle fell to Molly. It consumed her, filling the voids of loneliness, but it didn't give her pleasure.

That came from raising her only child, born out of wedlock when she was an 18-year-old farmer's daughter eager to leave home. Rather than put a ring on Molly's finger, the man abandoned her and the baby.

She met Withers two years later at the county fair. He was auctioning off a few steers and she was displaying her award-winning Dutch crumb apple pie. He bought her a Coke and asked her out. Their first date was a tour of his ranch.

He was eight years older. So rugged and handsome, so self-assured, so different than herself. His powerful aura consumed her. After a courtship that lasted just three weeks, he proposed. Hopelessly smitten, she said yes with tears in her eyes.

Johnny Caruso grew up tall and strong. Despite his mother's best efforts to steer him elsewhere, he dreamed of one day being either a soldier or a lawman, like his stepfather.

Withers had been elected sheriff by then, and Johnny was allowed to hang out in the office, where he heard the tales of grit and adventure spun by the older deputies. He learned to shoot and hunt, and helped Molly wrangle cows and run the ranch throughout his teenage years.

But when the time came for him to enter the police academy in Boise, she cried. How many more sleepless nights could she endure?

She made her husband promise to keep Johnny safe until she could convince him to pursue a less dangerous career. He reluctantly agreed.

Johnny became an Owyhee County deputy sheriff at the age of 21, destined to rise quickly through the ranks. His stepfather was a respected figure in the law enforcement community, and many of those top cops saw the same qualities in the earnest young man.

He had been on the job less than six months when the call went out about an armed robbery suspect on the run.

When the fugitive's stolen car was discovered in the enclave of Two Springs early the next morning, Caruso, who was off-duty at the time, was among the first deputies to respond.

His father liked to know in advance what he was doing, particularly in dangerous situations, but there was no time to wait. He longed for the chance to catch a fugitive and prove himself as more than just Frank Withers' boy.

As deputies fanned out to search the area at sunrise, knocking on doors and looking in woodsheds, he heard shouting and ran toward the commotion.

The fugitive was pinned down in a field behind a couple of homes. Caruso pulled his gun and advanced. He was 20 yards from the suspect, partially hidden in tall grass, when shots suddenly rang out – seemingly from all directions.

Moments later, a bullet struck Caruso in the throat and he fell to the ground.

Withers raced to the scene in time to see his stepson's body being lifted on a gurney and into an ambulance. The paramedic looked at the sheriff and shook his head sadly.

Stunned and full of rage, Withers strode over to Baker, who was on his knees and handcuffed, and punched him hard in the jaw.

"I'll kill you for this! I'll kill you for this!" he screamed, as his chief deputy wrapped him in a bear hug and dragged him away.

Hours passed before Withers could muster the courage to go home and pass the grim news on to his wife. He knew she'd fall apart, and he was not good at providing that kind of support.

When he opened the door and saw her face, he knew she had already been told.

Her round face was streaked with tears and her usually perfectly brushed brown hair was disheveled, as if she had been tearing at it.

"You did this," she said in an icy voice.

Those were the last words she would speak to him. That night, she moved her things out of their bedroom and slept in Johnny's old room. She didn't leave her husband so much as melt away, like a splintering glacier. When she collapsed in misery at her son's graveside, he was unable to console her.

Days passed and her despair only deepened. Withers begged her to get counseling. He called her closest relatives and pleaded with them to see her.

Molly would have none of it. Her grief was hers and hers alone.

Finally, on the tenth day, she poured herself a bath. She immersed her body in the warm water and rested the back of her head against the porcelain rim.

Then she ran a razor blade across her wrist and watched the water turn red with a dark joy. She'd be seeing her boy soon.

Withers found the body in the tub and fell to his knees. He pulled his wife's head to his chest and sobbed.

He was a powerful man, strong-willed and confident. But that day something inside of him snapped.

The impenetrable cloud of despair that had choked the life from his bride had entered him, like a parasite seeking a new host.

———

A blast from the ferry's horn broke the sheriff's spell.

He returned to his powerful truck. The rifle was behind the seat. A revolver was in the glove box.

He'd find his prey.

And vengeance would at last be served.

31

They slept together by the fire, huddled under a woven blanket.

At sunrise, Bud made some strong coffee and waited anxiously for Jo Jo to stir. He had important things to tell her. He wasn't afraid she'd leave him again – he just didn't want to scare her.

Not after all they'd been through. Not when he was on the verge of being truly free for the first time in his life. He knew now he couldn't achieve that blissful state of mind without her.

Jo Jo sat up and yawned. She turned and saw Bud in the breakfast nook. The table was a thick lacquered slice of cedar. A pair of carved stumps topped with cushions served as chairs.

"Thanks for keeping the fire going last night. Did you get enough sleep?"

"More than enough. Coffee's made."

"Thank God," she said, before dashing to the bathroom.

When she returned, Bud had the coffee poured in a touristy ceramic mug with the words "Kodiak-Emerald Isle" printed on it.

"Let's go shopping today!" she said brightly. "It'll be fun."

"Yes, dear," Bud said with a smile.

He lifted the knapsack from its peg on the wall and dumped the contents on the table, creating a heaping pile of hundred-dollar bills.

"Holy crap! Is that from the adoption center?" she asked, amazed.

"There was fifty thousand in three envelopes locked in the director's desk. Proof Jessie wasn't the only victim."

As Jo Jo ran her fingers lustily over the cash, he added: "There's about forty thousand left – I had to buy a car and hire a plane. When things calm down we should send Jessie half – for her restaurant."

"Wait a minute. Did you say 'buy a car and hire a plane?'"

"Baby, there's something I need to tell you. Try not to be too alarmed."

"Oh God. Now I *am* alarmed."

Bud stared at his girlfriend, saw the sudden panic on her face.

"There's no easy way to say it, so I'm just going to say it."

"Just tell me!"

"I'm being hunted."

"*What?*"

"By some nasty old dude. He thinks I killed his son 25 years ago – *I didn't, I swear* – and now that I'm out of prison he's hunting me down. He's coming here to finish the job."

"To Kodiak?"

Bud took a deep breath and nodded.

"A reporter I knew in Boise – the one who wrote the profile – left me a message at the general store. He said a former Idaho sheriff was on my tail, obsessed with revenge. He doesn't know where the cabin is, but he'll find it if he looks long and hard enough."

Jo Jo looked dazed. The color drained from her cheeks, making them seem even more pale than usual.

"His son was a deputy who was there when I was arrested. Shots were fired, but not by me. The boy was killed by friendly fire, but his father refuses to believe it. So, now I'm out and he's coming after me."

"Bud, maybe this tip is wrong," she said hopefully. "It can't be true. Hunt you from Idaho to Alaska?"

Bud shook his head.

"No, it makes sense. The night I left the adoption place, somebody shot at me. I got the hell out of there, heading north. The next day on the ocean highway, a big pickup truck rammed me from behind and sent me off a cliff. Sorry about your car, by the way. … I was lucky to survive both times."

"Oh my God!"

"I made it across the border and I saw the pickup again – in Canada! Finally, just a couple of days ago, I was making my way to Alaska when I saw that same truck on a hill overlooking the highway. I thought he was going to try to shoot me when I drove by. That's when I decided to pay a pilot to fly me here. So, no, I have no doubt he's crazy and hunting me like a goddamn trophy animal. I'm just sorry you're in the middle of it."

Jo Jo, deep in thought, cupped her chin with her hand.

"How much time do you think we have?"

"Before he finds us? A couple of days if we're lucky. I'm not known in town, but if he gets to old Sully … well, look how easily he helped you."

"And we can't go to the police."

"They're looking for us, too. If we show up at the station, they'll arrest us on the spot."

Bud searched for something soothing to say to his girlfriend when she surprised him with a determined look.

"That thing in the corner there," she said, pointing at the Remington leaning against a wall by the fireplace. "What is it?"

"You mean the shotgun?"

"Is it powerful?"

"It's a 12-gauge with double- 'ought buckshot, so yeah. I got it for hunting, but ..." Realizing why she was asking, his voice trailed off.

"Darling, teach me how to use it," she said, rising to her feet. "No crazy old man is going to hurt us."

———

The first practice shot knocked Jo Jo back a couple of feet. The second nearly hit the target, the beer bottle Bud placed on a stump about 50 feet away.

The third blew it to pieces.

"Great shooting, baby!"

"I think I get it," she said. "Let's go shopping."

"You think that's a good idea? I mean, what if he's in town, waiting?"

"I want real pillows and proper linens. And curtains. And shampoo and conditioner. Nobody better get in my way," she said, giving her meanest pretend look.

She handed Bud the gun. "Put this in the truck. I'll get the money bag. We've got some spending to do."

Bud started to protest, causing her to slip into the mean look again.

"Nobody get in my way!"

Bud's cabin was on the outskirts of Kodiak, near the northern edge of the federally protected wilderness that covered two-thirds of the island. As they drove into the town of 6,000 people, he pointed out a few restaurants that looked inviting.

"If we weren't Bonnie and Clyde, I'd force you to stop for a crab sandwich," she said, licking her lips.

"You wouldn't have to force me."

"Someday soon, right? When we're exonerated?"

"Someday soon."

They stopped at a couple of downtown stores and then Frontier Ridge for more supplies. After a couple of hours, they'd bought every item on Jo Jo's list, plus a few extras.

"I don't think we can squeeze anything else in," Bud said as he finished adding another bag to the bed of the pickup.

"I need beer," she said, ignoring him. "Where's the liquor store?"

"There, there and there," he said, pointing out several options. Liquor was big in Kodiak – the chest-warming antidote to long, snowy winters.

Bud emerged minutes later with a box of beer and booze that he squeezed between them on the Chevy's bench seat.

"Feel better?" he asked.

"Much."

Down the block, sitting on the bench outside the general store, a man in a cowboy hat was watching.

32

Judgment day.

With grim determination, Withers spurred the F-250 up a narrow, twisting road into dense forest. The eight-cylinder engine growled like a predator.

When the asphalt turned to gravel and then to dirt, he knew he was close.

The ancient, towering Sitka spruce parted slightly, and he caught a glimpse of deep blue below – a small lake with a fishing pier.

He had followed as Baker and his lady friend drove up the ridge. The dust they kicked up was his roadmap.

He pulled the Ford to the side. Stepping onto a crunching carpet of pine needles, he buckled a black leather holster around his waist and slid in a .38-caliber Smith & Wesson revolver, his old service weapon. The weight of the gun against his leg felt good. A trusted friend, long absent, had returned.

The hunt was nearly over after 2,700 miles and a few near misses.

Withers took his scoping sight from the truck and stuffed it in the pocket of the down vest over his blue flannel shirt.

He'd need to do some surveilling before he struck. He'd learned over many years not to leave much to chance.

He adjusted his Stetson, slid the Ray-Bans over his nose. Glancing in the truck's side mirror, he nodded his approval. The old cowboy was ready for one last ride.

For you, Molly.

For you, Johnny.

Withers weaved his way through thick underbrush and tree trunks until he could see the roof of a log cabin. White smoke billowed from the chimney.

Peering through the scope, he saw the rusted pickup parked in front. The truck's bed was empty.

That meant they were both probably inside. That meant justice, long delayed, would soon be delivered.

The presence of the woman complicated things, but only a little. He had no desire to hurt her. She was an innocent.

Baker was who he was after.

He drew his gun, checking to see that each of the six chambers was loaded.

He'd wait until his prey was outside and alone.

Then he'd strike and watch the bastard die.

Not for me.

For Molly and Johnny.

———

The men with insulated coats over their suits entered Frontier Ridge General Store and waited for the elderly owner to finish with a customer. After that man left with a 40-pound bag of rock salt slung over his shoulder, they walked up to the counter.

"Spencer Williams, FBI. This is Bellows," the special agent said, flashing his badge. His partner did the same.

"Feds. Here in Kodiak. Now that's something," Sullivan said, genuinely impressed.

"We're looking for someone. Wallace Baker, goes by Bud. Know where we can find him?" Williams said.

"I don't know, fellas. My memory is getting pretty bad. I'm almost 90 years old."

Williams gave a thin smile that wasn't friendly at all.

"Aiding and abetting a fugitive is a serious crime. Does that jog your memory?"

Sullivan sighed, triggering a brief coughing fit. He raised a hand to pause any more questions from the G-men while he wiped his wrinkled mouth with his ever-present handkerchief.

"I know Bud," he rasped. "I know he's in trouble."

The FBI agents exchanged glances.

"What have you heard?" Williams asked.

"That there's someone gunning for him. And I think he's here in town. Arrived today in a black pickup truck with Idaho plates."

"This person have a name?"

Sullivan shrugged.

"Can't help you there. I wasn't fooling when I said my memory ain't so good. A friend of Bud's from Boise called here to warn him. I made sure he got the message."

"Where is Baker now?" Bellows asked.

"They were in town this morning, getting more supplies. I suppose they went back to his cabin up the hill."

"Who is 'they'?"

"Bud and his girl. Very polite."

"What kind of supplies were they getting?"

"Oh, just some kitchen stuff. Utensils, hand soap, dish towels …"

"When was this?"

Sullivan glanced at the vintage Seiko watch that hung loosely from his bony wrist.

"Two hours ago, I reckon."

The agents asked for directions and Sullivan, in his shaking hand, drew a map on a scrap of paper.

Williams thanked the old man, who immediately lapsed into another coughing fit.

The agents had flown in by helicopter and had a silver Land Cruiser waiting when they arrived. As they headed up the hill toward Bud's cabin with Bellows behind the wheel a call was patched into Williams' phone. He put it on speaker.

"Williams."

"This is Johnson, from the Boise office," a man said. "I just got a call from a journalist at the local newspaper here. He said the former sheriff of Owyhee County is hunting one of your suspects. I thought you'd like to know."

"Thanks, any confirmation?"

"Afraid so. We did a little digging on this end and the sheriff – Frank Withers is his name – left his home a while ago and hasn't returned. There was a police report earlier this week that placed him in British Columbia. We think he's either in Kodiak now or heading there."

"That's an awfully long way to go. What is this Withers' motive?"

"We're not sure, but the journalist thinks he's obsessed with Wallace Baker, blames him for the death of his only son and his wife's subsequent suicide."

"When did that happen?"

"Twenty-five years ago, when Baker was arrested."

"Okay. We just arrived in Kodiak, talked to the old-timer who knows everyone in town, and sure enough he knows Baker. We're headed to his cabin now."

"Be careful. He's extremely dangerous."

"Baker?"

"No, Withers."

Williams hung up and looked at Bellows, who shook his head. What were they getting themselves into?

Bellows piloted the Land Cruiser through the woods as Williams navigated, using the crudely drawn map.

"Look," the driver said suddenly. "There's the truck. Idaho plates."

They parked behind the muddied Ford and stepped out, pulling their guns immediately.

"Tactical gear?" Bellows asked. "Call for back-up?"

"No time."

When they caught sight of the cabin, Williams stopped.

"You go around the back, I'll take the front," he told his partner, who was already on the move. "I have no idea what to expect, so be prepared to shoot."

As he slipped between the trees, the senior FBI agent cursed.

"Hell of a way to retire," he said.

33

Jo Jo finished making the new bed, with its white goose-down quilt and arrangement of lilac-colored pillows. The old brass headboard was polished and gleaming.

She backed up a couple of steps to take a look, hands on her hips.

"Not bad."

"Looks like a friggin' magazine!" exulted Bud, giving her a squeeze. "Amazing."

They walked together into the kitchen, where she had earlier unfurled a blue wool rug, hung some lacy white curtains and meticulously organized and lined the cupboards and drawers.

She stared at the slab-topped table and chiseled stump chairs and frowned.

"There's such a thing as too rustic."

"Never!"

"We'll see," she said, smiling.

"What's next, baby?"

They had bought a black wrought-iron wood rack, and it sat empty by the fireplace where logs were burning. She pointed at it and said to Bud, "Fill that, I guess. Does it ever get warm here?"

He laughed. It was mid-May and it still got frosty at night.

"You bet. For two weeks – in August. I'll chop some wood."

Jo Jo sidled up to him and gave him a kiss.

"And some wildflowers wouldn't hurt."

He grabbed her ass roughly, causing her to jump.

"Wallace!"

"Ugh, you know I hate that name."

"Yup, sure do."

"You're a terrible person."

"Yup, sure am."

Bud went to the front door and Jo Jo chased after him.

"Be careful," she said, looking worried. "Take the shotgun. Just in case."

"I'll have my axe. If he shows up, I'll chop him into pieces."

"Just be careful. *Please.*"

"I will."

"Promise me."

"I promise to be careful. I'll be right outside."

Bud stepped onto the wide porch and breathed in the sweet air. He didn't deserve a woman as strong as Jo Jo.

Anyone else would have been quaking in fear – or running away. Their lives were in danger, yet she insisted on going into town to shop. She knew the risk of staying, yet she did.

That took courage, he knew. A lot of it.

He grabbed the axe with its long wooden handle and red-and-silver blade and rested it against his shoulder like a lumberjack.

Whistling, he headed into the nearby woods.

———

Withers watched Baker leave the cabin.

Using his scoping sight, he could see the woman through the kitchen window. It looked like she was cleaning.

He watched Baker disappear between some trees. A minute or two later, the sheriff heard the sound of an axe biting into bark.

Perfect.

This is my chance to get the criminal alone.

Crouching, Withers worked his way closer to the cabin, using trees and bushes as cover.

He got to the edge of the clearing that fronted the homestead, partially covered in gravel. Then, in a final dash, he made it to the rear of the Chevy parked just off the porch.

Breathing hard, he sat with his back against the right rear wheel and pulled the revolver from its holster. Chopping sounds were still coming from the woods.

He'd be patient; wait for Baker to put down the axe.

Then he'd introduce himself.

And pronounce judgment.

———

As he threaded his way through the trees, Williams spotted the man in the cowboy hat.

Withers was hiding behind an old pickup, a gun in his right hand.

Williams crept closer and then could hear chopping sounds coming from the north side of the cabin, in a stand of pines. A man was whistling and it wasn't Withers.

He's going to ambush Baker.

This was not at all how the veteran agent wanted to close out a long and illustrious career – risking his life to confront a former lawman who had turned into a crazed vigilante.

He thought of his wife, two daughters and three grandchildren and uttered a silent prayer.

Staying hidden, Williams moved forward, his Glock at the ready. He was grateful that the chopping noise covered the sounds of twigs snapping under his shoes.

Moments later, the chopping stopped, replaced by a steady whistling.

The sheriff was getting ready to spring, but Williams was still too far away to get a clean shot.

And then Baker, arms full of firewood, stepped into the clearing.

34

Jo Jo saw the man who was hunting them through the window. He was hiding behind the pickup, but she could see the top of his hat.

Bud!

She ran to the next room and grabbed the shotgun and the box of shells from the mantle.

Hustling back to the window, she saw the hunter starting to slowly rise. The sun glinted off the barrel of his gun.

And then she heard Bud's whistles growing louder. He was walking into a trap!

Jo Jo started to load the gun, but her hands were shaking and the shells fell clumsily to the floor. She scooped them up and tried again.

Then she heard voices.

———

Withers popped out from behind the truck, his revolver aimed at Bud's head.

An eerie smile spread across the sheriff's leathery face.

Stunned, Bud dropped the wood. He was in the middle of the clearing with no cover – defenseless as a big man in a cowboy hat had him trapped at point-blank range.

Bud raised his hands in the air and gulped.

Was this how it would end for him? Gunned down on his own property after getting a tantalizing taste of freedom? A second chance at love?

"Baker," the man said in his gravelly voice. "There's no escaping now."

It's judgment day.

"Withers?"

"Remember me from your parole hearings?"

"That's kinda fuzzy. I remember you more from the punch in the jaw."

Withers' look hardened.

"Make all the jokes you want. They'll be your last. I just want you to die knowing why."

"I didn't kill your boy," Bud pleaded, hands still raised. "I never fired my gun that day, and you know it. You saw the reports."

The sheriff spit in disgust.

"Johnny wouldn't have died if it weren't for you, you sonofabitch. And my Molly, she took her life days after. You caused all that."

Withers' sun-baked face reddened with anger as his finger gripped the trigger.

"Easy," Bud said softly. "Your son's death, it was an accident. One of your deputies fired that shot."

"Take it to your grave, convict. I just wanted to look you in the eye when I put a bullet in your brain."

The cabin door suddenly swung open. Jo Jo took one step onto the porch, leveling the shotgun at Withers.

"Leave him alone!" she yelled.

The fugitive hunter – his instincts kicking in – wheeled and fired.

The bullet struck Jo Jo above her chest, and she collapsed like a paper doll. The shotgun fell from her hands with a thud.

"No!!"

Bud ran to her. Blood was flowing and her arms and legs were twitching.

The sheriff froze. The look on his face changed, as if he was seeing through his madness for a moment.

"FBI! Drop the gun!" Williams shouted, stepping out of the brush.

In a blink of an eye, Withers crouched and spun around, firing the revolver in a fluid motion.

Almost as fast, Williams squeezed the trigger of his Glock, sending a bullet whizzing over the sheriff's right shoulder. A split second earlier, it would have pierced the man's heart.

Then the FBI agent cried out in pain. The sheriff's bullet had struck his right hand, causing him to drop the gun.

As Withers took aim at the suddenly unarmed Williams, about to fire the fatal shot, there was a loud blast.

Withers yelled and arched his back.

The would-be assassin tottered, then slowly fell face-first to the ground, hat tumbling to his side.

Williams looked up and saw Bud standing on the porch with the shotgun, its barrel smoking.

Bud dropped the weapon. He pulled off his neckerchief and held it against Jo Jo's wound, trying to stop the bleeding.

"Call an ambulance!" he shouted. Bellows, now in the clearing, pulled out his phone.

Williams, clutching his injured hand, used his foot to roll over Withers. He was taking his last breaths.

"Molly," he said through clenched teeth. "Forgive ... me."

35

Bud sat next to Jo Jo in the Anchorage hospital room, holding her limp hand. His shirt, already stained by her blood, was now wet with his tears.

After an emergency flight from Kodiak and more than five hours of surgery, doctors were short on answers. She had lost too much blood and had slipped into a coma, they said.

The gunman's bullet struck her spine and there was a chance that, even if she survived, she'd be completely paralyzed.

The free-spirited woman who seemed to float on air could be lost to Bud forever.

Those thoughts were tormenting him when the door to the intensive-care room opened and Williams walked in, dressed as usual in a nice suit. The bandage on his wrist was the only clue that he'd just survived a brush with death.

Bud looked up and grimaced. He knew he'd committed too many crimes to not pay a price.

"I suppose you know all about the baby."

"We do. And the couple you tied up in the basement."

"Right."

Williams took a seat and smoothed his thin mustache. The men looked at each other across Jo Jo's body as the ventilator thumped and monitors beeped.

"We got your extremely detailed tip about the black-market operation," Williams said. "Thanks for that."

There was silence that stretched for minutes, except for the beeping and thumping.

"Why'd you do it?" Williams said finally. "You could have grabbed the baby and fled. Why send us that information? Why call the police on yourself?"

Bud shrugged. He had asked himself those very questions many times.

"I'm not a criminal, man. I mean I *was*, but that's not who I want to be. When I became a jailhouse lawyer, I changed. I actually enjoyed helping other people for the first time in my life. Surprise, surprise. So, when Jo told me about her sister and the baby, I was torn. I didn't want to go back to prison, not after finally getting out. Not after 25 years. I wanted to go straight in the worst way.

"I was having nightmares and stress attacks and shit. I think it was my brain and body warning me, telling me not to do any more crimes. But then I met Jessie and I saw the terrible harm they did to her. And I … well, I had to set things right. Does that make sense?"

"Sure. But the former sheriff didn't get the message. He was hunting the old Bud."

"Suppose so."

"I prefer the new Bud. With your help, we found other birth mothers who had their babies stolen from them. Most of the women were addicts or developmentally disabled. A lot of money changed hands."

"I knew there was more to it than just Jessie's baby."

Williams stood and Bud flinched. He wished he had more time to hold vigil, to study Jo Jo's perfect face.

"I shouldn't tell you this, but the case is before a federal grand jury," Williams said. "We expect indictments soon — the director and a half-dozen co-conspirators, including a top police official and deputy mayor."

"They deserve what's coming to them. What will happen to Jessie and her baby?"

"Oh, nothing. She's a star witness. The adoptive parents were surprisingly understanding about her coming forward as a victim. Of course, they've been moved to the top of the list at a legitimate adoption agency and they're about to sue Little Angels for a few million, so that should ease their suffering."

"And what about Jo Jo? If she makes it, I mean."

"She'll be free to go. But you really should be asking about yourself."

Bellows popped his head in the doorway.

"Spencer, the plane's here. We should leave soon if we're going to make it to Portland," he said.

Williams nodded. "I'll be right there."

Bellows left and the soon-to-be-retired investigator gave Bud a penetrating look.

"You know you risked it all, right? Your freedom, everything, for a couple of women you barely knew."

"Yeah, I know. Crazy, huh?"

Williams shrugged. It wasn't for him to say.

"Hey, I didn't thank you for saving my life back there. Withers had the drop on me."

"Well, you were trying to save mine. So that makes us even, I guess.

"I guess it does."

Bud walked over to Williams. He extended his arms like he had done so many times behind bars.

"Get it over with."

Williams hesitated for a few seconds before handcuffing Bud's wrists.

"I'm sorry, but there's no way a man who kidnaps a baby at gunpoint can just walk. No matter how justified it may seem."

"I know, man. I guess I knew it all along."

The FBI agent put a hand on Bud's shoulder and looked him in the eyes.

"But if you're a cooperating witness in the Little Angels case, I'm sure I can convince the U.S. Attorney's Office to recommend a reduced sentence – say, one year at a minimum-security federal prison, minus time off for good behavior."

Bud seemed surprised. He knew how different the federal lockup would be compared to the gritty Idaho State Penitentiary with its hardened cons and Death Row.

"I'll do it."

"I was hoping you'd say that. But I do have a question."

"Go ahead."

"The adoption center in Astoria reported a burglary that happened the night you stole the baby. They didn't disclose that anything valuable was taken, but they were raking in a lot of money. Know anything about that?"

Bud thought about the loot he and Jo Jo buried behind the cabin – the nest egg for themselves and Jessie.

"Nope. Not a clue."

Williams, one of the bureau's keenest minds, grinned.

"We'll go with that," he said.

His face turned serious as he glanced down at Jo Jo. "You better say your goodbye."

Bud returned to his bedside chair. He wanted so badly to tell his love the news: They really did have a future together.

Once he got out of prison a second time. And if she could claw her way back from the darkness.

He kissed her cheek and clasped his hands together.

For the first time in his life, he prayed.

36

In the end, Anna Kendrall refused to be silenced.

The maternity ward nurse's stunning insider testimony before a federal grand jury would prove instrumental in bringing down the Little Angels baby-peddling operation.

It would also expose an insidious web of people profiting off the misfortune and misery of others while convincing themselves it was for the greater good.

Through such a distorted lens, taking healthy babies from addicts and the cognitively impaired, and giving them to loving, barren couples who had the means to raise them properly, seemed like a Christian thing to do.

Kendrall's defection was viewed by Krump and the others with more pity than panic. Had the nurse lost her faith?

The truth was Kendrall, who at 42 was divorced with no children, fled Astoria after suffering too long from a guilty conscience.

She tipped off the family of the latest victim, a heroin addict and her sister, and hightailed it down to Texas, where she attempted to start over at a small pregnancy clinic in Waco.

The schemers found her quickly, as she had feared, knowing that the Oregon city's top police detective was in on it. Perhaps lacking the religious fervor of his co-conspirators, he strongly advised Kendrall to keep her mouth shut.

"We know how to find you," the cop said. "There's no place you can hide."

Weeks passed before a man in a suit appeared at the clinic. He showed the nurse his badge and they went into a small conference room to talk.

"Ms. Kendrall, you've been implicated in a criminal scheme," Spencer Williams began.

Before the FBI agent could say another word, she began to cry.

"I know, I know."

Williams handed her his handkerchief. She waived her rights and immediately began telling her harrowing story.

Kendrall had been involved in four cases in which babies had been taken from their birth mothers. Jessie Summers was the only one who arrived in a stupor. The others were developmentally disabled and easily misled.

Those women were living independently, some even holding jobs, but they remained under an umbrella of state and federal agencies and received monthly disability benefits.

Over a number of years, Little Angels had wormed its way into a state-funded program for developmentally disabled adults in Astoria in which pregnant clients had to prove themselves capable of parenting.

The adoption agency, through its surrogates, made it impossible for anyone to make the grade.

Their babies were taken away at birth and placed in temporary foster homes that soon led to permanent placements. The birth mothers, many of them only mildly impaired, were told, at the end of a torturous gauntlet of "classes," that they were incapable of mothering. They had failed.

They were not, however, incapable of sorrow. Almost all went through agonizing heartbreak after losing their babies – a fact that never made it into any of the reports filed in family court.

The pipeline served Little Angels well, since virtually all of the babies were born healthy, both physically and mentally, and the program made no effort to provide its female clients with birth control or sex education.

The scheme also targeted pregnant women who abused drugs, but that called for a different strategy. A few surrendered their newborns at the hospital, persuaded that they were unable to provide a suitable home. If any arrived at the maternity ward under the influence, the stillborn lie could be used.

As the babies kept coming and cash donations from grateful adoptive parents rolled in, everybody, including Kendrall, took a cut.

The worst part of it all, the nurse told Williams, was the look on the mothers' faces.

"I can't describe it in words," she said, still clutching the handkerchief. "The amount of pain we caused, *I* caused … it's beyond comprehension. After lying to Jessie Summers, that was it. My breaking point.

"The horror in her eyes. I'll never forget it."

She paused a moment to collect herself, then continued.

"I delivered her baby to Little Angels and then I left. I couldn't do it anymore. There was too much agony."

They talked for another hour before Williams gave her an ultimatum. "If you testify fully, I'll make sure you get immunity. Otherwise, I'll have to arrest you like the others," he said.

Kendrall nodded solemnly.

"I knew this day would come. Yes, I'll testify. Will Jessie be there?"

"She's also a witness, so yes."

"Good," the nurse said.

———

Deep inside the federal courthouse in Portland, Jessie emerged from the room where grand jurors hear closed-door testimony.

Prosecutors relied heavily on her account. She was one of the few victims of the baby-stealing plot capable of describing the crime and its aftermath in gut-wrenching terms.

The experience was cathartic in many ways, and as the woman from the U.S. Attorney's Office victims' assistance unit handed Patrick back to her, she wished other mothers snared in the scheme could also find some peace.

It helped to see the front page of the Oregonian with the banner headline: "Exclusive: FBI Probes Baby-Selling

Adoption Agency." There was a big picture of Krump, trying unsuccessfully to shield her face from the camera.

Jessie smiled, knowing Bud's meticulous planning had paid off.

Waiting for the elevator, her ebullient son on her hip, she felt eager to return home, her brief stint as a fugitive officially a thing of the past.

Then she looked up and gasped.

The woman who stole her baby was standing a few feet away.

"I'm so happy to see you with your son," Kendrall said. "I'm sorry—"

Jessie cut her off.

"After what you did to me, you think you can just say you're sorry?"

Kendrall bowed her head.

"No, of course, not. I'll never forgive myself. I just wanted you to know that."

"I know that you testified. That's something at least, but forgiveness is something I can never give you."

"Seeing you with your baby is enough. I'm sorry to have disturbed you."

Kendrall began to walk away, but Jessie stopped her.

"Wait, come here. This is Patrick," the mother said. She held him up in his onesie, his chubby little legs dangling.

"This is the baby you stole from me and had sold, like a damn beagle."

Then she pulled down her scarf to reveal a long red mark on her neck, a chilling reminder of her suicide attempt.

It was a scar she'd kept hidden from everyone, even her sister. But for this woman, Jessie made an exception.

"I nearly hanged myself because of you," she seethed.

The disgraced nurse broke into sobs, slumping against the cold courthouse walls. The mournful sound echoed down the hall, causing people to stop and stare.

The bronze elevator doors opened with a ding.

"*Now* you understand," Jessie said, stepping inside.

37

A man in a rumpled navy blazer walked past bustling tennis courts on a pleasant autumn afternoon in upstate New York.

He entered the adjoining, one-story building and was escorted past the pool tables and cafeteria lined with vending machines to a small conference room furnished with a polished-wood table and padded chairs.

The minimum-security federal camp in Otisville was a far cry from the Boise prison, with its razor wire, attack dogs and sharpshooters. For one thing, there were no security fences or barred cells.

Otisville had become famous for housing high-profile hucksters who did their time in relative comfort, including a number of men convicted of insider trading and corporate fraud.

Inmates who behaved got unguarded furloughs to visit their families, a huge perk. A library offered slightly dated music CDs and bestselling books. Sleeping quarters were dorm-style with bunks, and the showers featured individual stalls. A gym had treadmills and exercise bikes. There were even tennis courts and a softball field.

"Good for you, Bud," Sweet said to himself as he laid down his shoulder bag and took out a notebook and voice recorder.

Williams had chosen Otisville for Bud as one of his final acts as an FBI hero. True to his word, he also convinced prosecutors to recommend a one-year sentence. The judge accepted it, citing Bud's cooperation and good intentions.

Bud was now only a few months from getting out, and Sweet decided it was time to do a final in-person interview.

The inmate walked in, smiled broadly and gave the reporter a big hug. There was no Plexiglass to keep them apart, no corrections officer keeping watch.

"Roger, my man," Bud said.

"My favorite convict," Sweet replied.

"Ready to fill up some more notebooks?"

"Not as many as before. I have this now."

The journalist tapped his sleek digital device, which he turned on.

"Sorry to drag you all the way to New York, but I'm happy you came," Bud said. "There are no federal lockups in Alaska and prisons in the Northwest aren't as nice, so here I am – thousands of miles from home."

"Thanks for your letter. It filled a lot of blanks. Sorry to hear that your girlfriend was shot by the crazy sheriff. What's the latest on her condition?"

Bud pursed his lips. His eyes misted.

"I'm not sure," he said.

After he cooperated with federal prosecutors, fulfilling his agreement, Bud tried desperately to get updates on Jo Jo. He called the Anchorage hospital every day, and staffers told him nothing had changed – she was still in a coma on life support.

Then one day, after he had been at Otisville for about a month, the nurse in charge said Jo Jo was alert and in stable condition.

Bud rejoiced at the news and asked for the call to be forwarded to Jo Jo's room, but after a pause the nurse got back on the line and said the patient was too tired to talk.

The next day, and the day after that, Bud was told the same thing.

And then, finally, the nurse on the phone said Jo Jo didn't want to be disturbed.

"What does that mean?" Bud asked.

The nurse sighed. "She can't walk. That may not change."

"I don't care about that. I love her. Why won't she talk to me?"

"Sweetie," the woman said, "she thinks she's doing you a favor."

"What favor?"

"A chance for you to move on."

Staggered, Bud hung up. In his heart, he knew her physical condition didn't matter. He'd love her no matter what.

But how could he persuade Jo Jo if she wouldn't take his calls?

He wrote several long and passionate letters and when he received nothing in response, he again called the hospital.

The nurse he had spoken with earlier told him Jo Jo refused to read the heartfelt messages. She also confided that the patient had been discharged to a nearby live-in rehabilitation center, where she was receiving physical therapy every day.

Supervisors at that center weren't as kind as the nurse. When Bud called a second time, they told him to stop. The patient didn't want to talk. At her request, they refused to provide any more information.

He had lost his connection to her.

Doing his best to hold back tears, Bud poured out his heart to Sweet. Then he asked the journalist to do him a favor.

"Please put that in your story and send a copy to Jo Jo. If she'll take your call, tell her I'm getting out soon and hope to see her in Kodiak, by the lake."

Sweet nodded. "Eighty-nine days, right?"

"That's right. Free again in eighty-nine days."

Later, Sweet asked the tough questions that forced Bud to delve deeply into his vault of feelings.

"Bud, you may be the only man in history who stole a baby that had already been stolen. I know you've called it a 'righteous' crime, but now you're back in prison after nearly getting killed. Was it worth it?"

"Yeah, I'd do it again," the inmate said. "And I have proof that I made the right decision."

"What proof?"

"Since I've been here I haven't had a single nightmare. I used to wake up in cold sweats at the ISP. When I got out, I had these awful, body-shaking flashbacks. But now it's all over. I can sleep again."

"So, your conscience is no longer haunting you?"

"Something like that. But there's another reason I know I made the right decision: Soon, I hope, I'll be going home to Jo Jo."

Sweet scribbled away in his shorthand and Bud watched approvingly.

"Is this for the Idaho paper?"

The reporter chuckled.

"And *Rolling Stone* and The New York Times and a few others. You're a hot commodity, Bud. I hear you've gotten interview requests from all the TV networks. Why did you turn them down?"

Bud strapped his arms across his chest.

"I only talk to Roger Sweet, the man who helped save my life. Those other people, they just want to make money or get big ratings. Screw them."

For a moment, the men sat in silence, smiling at each other in mutual admiration.

"Now come on, lightweight," Bud said. "What's your next question?"

38

Bud stood beside the ice-blue lake, savoring the splendor before him.

The sun was slipping behind the tall trees, the sky turning pink like cotton candy. A large fish breached the surface, causing ripples to gently wash against the shore. On the ridge above he saw the silhouette of a shaggy bear.

Tomorrow, he'd bring his pole and some bait. That would be nice, he thought. Maybe light the grill after, cook some trout.

It was a warm summer evening, and there was no need to go anywhere or do anything. Except this one thing.

One lovely thing.

For the mermaid.

Standing next to a small rowboat, she tossed aside her crutches. He guided her onto one of the wooden seats and together they glided to the center of the lake, where the colors above were the most brilliant.

Jo Jo stared in wonder, green eyes sparkling. A breeze ruffled her fiery tresses like a friendly spirit.

Bud watched her, also in wonder.

"You look so beautiful," he said.

She smiled. Bud looked so much younger now that his soul was truly free.

"Whistle for me, darling," she said.

AUTHOR'S NOTE

Let's get right to it. There really was a Bud. Maybe *is*. I'm not sure.

I lost track of Walter "Bud" Balla shortly after he was released from the Idaho State Penitentiary in the middle of the night many years ago after being a pain-in-the-ass jailhouse lawyer. I was then a reporter covering courts for the Idaho Statesman in Boise.

Bud, suddenly bound for Kodiak, Alaska, called me from the airport. "I'm free and I don't know how to act," he said.

That's all I can tell you. He could be dead, back behind bars or out there somewhere in the woods. It would be awesome to hear from him again – to thank him for sparking my first novel – but either way, I'm giving him his due: While this book flows from my imagination, the inspiration behind the protagonist is real.

There are many others who helped make this book a reality.

I want to thank my love Ann Butler for the kind words and gentle nudges that were the wind at my back.

I am also deeply appreciative of my childhood pal John Brush for his critiques and journalist Bridget Murphy for her consultations and line edit.

To my readers who offered invaluable feedback and support, I am further indebted: Jesse Miller; Jacob Miller; Jim Floyd; Scott Palfreeman; Bruce Andrews; and Denise Brush. In addition, I am grateful for the help of Kimi Miller, whose marketing wizardry expanded this book's reach.

Finally, a shout-out to Astoria, Oregon, my new hometown, for giving me a quirky setting for a quirky tale.